eur—*Fleur*! What is it?'

ßastian strode right over to
˙ bed, and without a second's
sitation she sprang up into a
ıeeling position and clutched
m feverishly around the neck.

ıd with that human contact, feeling the com-
rting warmth of his bare chest against her flim-
y clad form, she burst into tears.

bastian let her do it, saying not another word,
t sitting down on the bed with her, his arms
apped around her, his chin resting on the top
her head.

ush, Fleur…it's OK…you're OK. I'm here…'
murmured.

terwards, she couldn't recall how long they'd
yed like that, but eventually she raised her
s to look up at him. And then, as if it were the
ious, natural sequence of events, his mouth
ame down upon her lips. And the moist warmth
of that brief union sent thrilling waves coursing
down her spine… She didn't pull away—she
didn't *want* to pull away. Because in a kind of
wonder she   s intimate

                                              mak-

Susanne James has enjoyed creative writing since childhood, completing her first—sadly unpublished—novel by the age of twelve. She has three grown-up children who were, and are, her pride and joy, and who all live happily in Oxfordshire with their families. She was always happy to put the needs of her family before her ambition to write seriously, although along the way some published articles for magazines and newspapers helped to keep the dream alive!

Susanne's big regret is that her beloved husband is no longer here to share the pleasure of her recent success. She now shares her life with Toffee, her young Cavalier King Charles spaniel, who decides when it's time to get up (early) and when a walk in the park is overdue!

Recent titles by the same author:

THE BRITISH BILLIONAIRE'S INNOCENT BRIDE
THE MILLIONAIRE'S CHOSEN BRIDE
THE BRITISH BILLIONAIRE AFFAIR
JED HUNTER'S RELUCTANT BRIDE

THE PLAYBOY OF PENGARROTH HALL

BY
SUSANNE JAMES

MILLS & BOON
Pure reading pleasure™

All the characters in this book have no existence outside the imagination
of the author, and have no relation whatsoever to anyone bearing the
same name or names. They are not even distantly inspired by any
individual known or unknown to the author, and all the incidents are
pure invention.

THE PLAYBOY OF
PENGARROTH HALL

For Kathie,
a true friend.

CHAPTER ONE

THIS just had to be paradise, Fleur thought, as she trod her way carefully through the extensive grounds of Pengarroth Hall, her feet crunching through the undergrowth. A pale December sun filtering through the naked branches of the tall trees towering all around had not yet managed to thaw the dainty traces of frost glistening everywhere—but, if *this* was beautiful, what must spring and summer be like, with everything alive and in full leaf? the girl thought.

Finding the first gated entrance she'd come to locked, she had decided to walk, and had been going for some time before realizing that there had to be a more obvious route to the house than this. The path she'd started along had seemed established enough at first but had gradually petered out, but it was such a beautifully restful area in which to stroll, she'd decided to keep going just to enjoy being out of the car after her long drive from London and breathe in this fresh country air. She'd retrace her steps in a minute, she thought, and drive further on down the hill. Mia, the friend who'd invited her to spend Christmas here in the family home she shared with her brother, had been characteristically vague with her instructions.

"Just drive through the first big gate you come to," she'd said airily. "You can't miss it."

A little later, and with a painful stab of anxiety, Fleur recognized the familiar prickling at the back of her neck which usually heralded one of her bouts of exhaustion, and she kicked herself for being an idiot. She knew that if she wanted to stay well, she had to take care of herself, and she knew she had been overdoing it in the run-up to Christmas. They'd been working late at the laboratory for the last two weeks, and today's long drive to Cornwall hadn't helped. It would have been better to have waited until tomorrow, Christmas Eve, before leaving London, but Mia had persuaded her to come a day early.

"None of the other guests will have arrived, and my darling brother won't be there either, not until Christmas morning, so we'll have the house to ourselves," she'd enthused. "It'll be like old times in the dorm!" The two girls had been at the same boarding school and had remained firm friends ever since, though this was the first time Fleur had visited Pengarroth Hall.

Spotting a flat tree trunk just in front of her, Fleur sat down on it gingerly—she knew she wouldn't be able to stay there long because it was clearly very cold and damp, but it would do for her to rest there for just a few moments. She glanced at her watch—it was four o'clock already and starting to get dark—before closing her eyes briefly.

Suddenly, from out of nowhere and causing her to jump, a strong voice interrupted her thoughts.

'Good afternoon. Can I help you?'

The enquiry was brusque, with no hint of Christmas cheer about it, and Fleur looked up quickly, scrambling to her feet. She was confronted by a tall man wearing a mud-smeared wax jacket and heavy boots—and a rather forbidding expression on what was clearly a very handsome face. A shotgun hung over his shoulder. His eyes were darkly penetrating as they stared down at her, and she couldn't help feeling a tremor of apprehension—mixed with something else she was not going to acknowledge!—as she returned his gaze. Then she straightened her back, and she smiled—obviously this was the gamekeeper, or some other person employed at Pengarroth Hall.

'I don't need any help at all, thanks,' she said brightly. 'I've been enjoying a stroll in these wonderful woods, that's all.'

He didn't answer for a moment, unable to drag his gaze from the most delectable female features he'd seen in a long time. Then, 'Well, you are on private property. This area is not open for walkers. The public right of way is much further back up the hill,' he said bluntly. 'The notice is clearly marked.'

Fleur bristled at this show of pomposity. There was no need to be quite so horrible about it, even if she had been trespassing which, as an invited guest, was not the case. She attempted a thin smile, irritated with him now and not wanting to reveal that she was going to be staying at the house, or that she was a long-time friend of one of the owners.

'Oh, really?' she said. 'I really must be more careful where I put my size threes, mustn't I.' She glanced at the gun. 'Do you shoot trespassers?'

His firm mouth twisted slightly at the question, and he pushed a damp stray lock of dark hair back from his forehead. 'I'd better show you the way back in case you get lost. There are several different paths,' he said.

Fleur stared at him coldly. She could rely on her own brain

and sense of direction, thank you. She certainly didn't want any favours from this surly individual. 'Don't bother yourself. I don't need any guidance, thank you,' she said tightly.

'Well, daylight will be gone soon,' he said. 'Please make your way back to the road.' He looked straight down into her cool green eyes before adding, 'This section of the grounds is being restored—blight damage to some of the trees has meant considerable replanting, and we don't want the new saplings to be disturbed by people tramping where they shouldn't.' Then he nodded briefly, turned around and walked away without another word.

Well, Fleur thought as she watched him disappearing through the gathering gloom, she'd give him ten out of ten for carrying out his duties. He'd certainly put *her* in her place. Say what you mean, and mean what you say—a man after her father's heart, that was for sure! She shook her head briefly as she thought of her parents—Helen and Philip—who were, unusually, spending Christmas in Boston this year. She couldn't remember a time when they'd not all spent the festive season together at home. But Professor Richardson, a renowned lecturer in mathematics, had seized an opportunity to mix business with pleasure, so the usual family plans had been changed.

She retraced her steps, making sure she was going the right way. It was obviously her own fault that she'd fallen foul of Mia's vague directions, and she'd known almost straight away that the path she'd chosen was not the one which would lead to the house. But she'd thoroughly enjoyed her stroll in the woods—shame that she'd had to meet up with the dour groundsman and spoil it.

It was now practically dark by the time she got back to the car. No wonder the gate had been locked—it was a wonder that they hadn't put coils of barbed wire all around it to keep everyone out!

Half a mile further down the hill, Pengarroth Hall came into view, and as Fleur approached she saw the gate which Mia had said she couldn't miss. It was wide open and inviting and, making her way slowly up the curving drive to the front door, she felt a rush of renewed pleasure at the thought of being somewhere different, with different people, for the holiday. Mia had said she'd invited several other friends along as well.

"The only one you'll have met before is Mandy,' Mia had said on the phone. 'Remember Mandy? She's a real laugh.'

Oh, I remember Mandy, Fleur had thought, a total man-eater, but yes, she'd be fun.

'All the others work with me at the office, but I promise not to allow any shop talk,' Mia had said. Mia was em-ployed by a very successful PR company in London—a far cry from Fleur's research work in one of the city's teaching hospitals. Although their lives had taken such different paths since school and university days, they had never lost touch, and it was Mia's free and easy personal life, uncon-strained by the wishes of demanding parents, that had caused Fleur many pangs of envy. Philip Richardson had had such plans for his only child—it had never occurred to him that she might have had some ambitions of her own. But, dutifully, Fleur had attained her science degree, as he'd directed, and was also careful not to introduce too many boyfriends to her parents. Not that her mother would have objected but, like Fleur, the woman was in thrall to the intellect and influence of the man in their lives, and both of them did their best not to cross him.

Now, in answer to the clanging of the ancient bell, the

door was opened by a tall, rather straight-faced woman in her mid-fifties, Fleur guessed, but her broad smile was engaging enough as she introduced herself quickly.

'Oh, hello. I'm Pat—I'm housekeeper here,' she introduced herself.

'Hi, I'm Fleur Richardson.' Fleur smiled back.

'Yes, I was told you'd be the only one arriving today. Do come in. You obviously found us all right.' She stood aside as Fleur entered. 'Mia's washing her hair,' she added. 'I'll tell her you're here.'

As soon as she set foot in the place, Fleur knew that Pengarroth Hall was a home in every sense of the word. She was aware that the building was more than two hundred years old and had been owned by Mia's family for four generations, but it felt beautifully warm, cosy and welcoming. The entrance hall where she was standing was enhanced by a gigantic Christmas tree, glistening with tinsel, baubles and lights, standing at the foot of the wide staircase. In the corner was a huge grandfather clock, along the walls were a couple of low sofas, a well-worn table with some daily papers scattered about and in another corner on a low armchair a very old black Labrador snoozed, its grey-whiskered jaws and body almost lost amongst the squashy folds of an ancient blue velvet cushion. When it became aware that Fleur was standing there, the animal opened one eye, took a long deep breath, then went back to sleep. Fleur couldn't help smiling. How different all this was from her parents' well-kept mid-thirties house in Surrey—to say nothing of her own smart London flat. But she felt almost embraced by the atmosphere here, and knew she was going to love every minute of the holiday.

Just then, Mia appeared at the top of the stairs,

wearing only her bra and pants, her head swathed in a large white towel.

'Hi-ya Fleur! Come on up—shan't be a jiff. Isn't this fun? I *love* Christmas!'

Happily, Fleur did as she was told, sitting on the edge of Mia's bed as Mia began rubbing her hair briskly.

'I hope you don't mind sharing my room,' Mia said breathlessly, 'and I'm asking the others to share as well.' She peered out from among the folds of the towel. 'It's not that there aren't enough rooms to go around in this place, of course, but I didn't like to give Pat all the extra work. And I know the boys won't mind sharing—you'll like them, Fleur. Gus and Tim are old friends in any case, and Rupert and Mat are really nice.' She draped the towel over the back of a chair and reached for her hairdryer.

'Of course I don't mind sharing,' Fleur said at once. 'It'll be like old times.' She paused. 'Your hair's grown so long, Mia. I've never seen it like that.'

Mia was strikingly tall, and her dark brown hair, reaching well below her shoulders, made her seem even taller. Her hazel eyes twinkled.

'Well, that's Mat's fault. He likes it this way,' she said, switching on the dryer.

Fleur raised her eyebrows. 'Oh? So Mat is—important—is he? The man of the moment?'

Mia smiled briefly. 'Sort of,' she said vaguely. 'We've been going out for a bit—nothing too heavy. In fact, I thought it wise to mix him up with others for Christmas—before we both get carried away.' She paused. 'What about you—anyone special on the scene?' She raised her voice slightly above the noise of the dryer.

'No, there isn't,' Fleur replied flatly. And probably never

will be, she could have added, but didn't. Mia shot her an understanding glance, but said nothing. She knew that Fleur's father had always discouraged his daughter from having relationships. 'Don't waste your intelligence and education on marriage and children,' was his frequent advice to his daughter. 'There's plenty of time for that.'

'Well, let me remind you that next year we're both going to be twenty-seven,' Mia said, somewhat ruefully. 'Not that our biological clocks are running out exactly, but time does seem to be on wheels, doesn't it?' She switched off the dryer for a second and sighed. 'I love the idea of marriage and a family, but finding the right partner seems an impossible task. As soon as I get to know someone, really get to know how he ticks, I lose interest.' She gave a short laugh. 'It's obviously all *my* fault.' She waited a second before going on. 'Has there been anyone special since you and Leo split up?'

Fleur shrugged, looking away. 'No, not really. A few of us from work get together fairly regularly for drinks or a night out somewhere, but I always go home alone, like the good girl that I am.' Her lip curled slightly as she made that remark. Looking back on her time with Leo, when they'd meant so much to each other, she couldn't believe, now, that she'd allowed her father to come between them. But in the three years that had elapsed since that time, she'd come to realize that it had all been for the best, after all. Because she'd become utterly convinced that marriage was not for her. She would never risk being in the position which her mother had occupied all *her* life—to be subservient, having to fall in with every wish of her husband's. Although Fleur acknowledged that he was basically a good man, he had totally domineered his wife—and his daughter—because there was only one opinion that mattered: his own. And he could never accept that he might sometimes be wrong, or that others might be right. With her reasoning, analytical, intellect, Fleur know that it was fundamentally wrong for one human being—whoever he was—to always have his own way, and that she would never put up with that state of affairs.

She got up and went over to the window, gazing out across the garden and the woods beyond.

Mia, sensing her sudden sadness, said cheerfully, 'Well, unfortunately for the rest of us, when we were all young and innocent, you were the one that the guys all fancied, and we were very jealous, I can tell you. I don't know how you've managed to stay single for so long, Fleur Richardson, I really don't.'

It was true that Fleur had always been attractive to men, her dainty figure and heart-shaped face dominated by thickly lashed large green eyes crying out for attention and admiration. Plus those two other seductive characteristics—a high intelligence coupled with a teasingly vulnerable nature making men automatically feel protective towards her.

'Oh, there's nothing to it—staying single, I mean,' Fleur replied. 'Just keep your head down and go on working. There's always—*always*—stuff waiting to be done in the lab. Stuff that can't wait.' Besides,' she added, 'in my experience, men always seem to need to be in control all the time…and I want to be in control of my own life, thanks very much.'

'Some of them do,' Mia agreed, 'but there are ways of dealing with that. A little feminine cunning and you can often bring them around to your way of thinking.'

'Hmm,' Fleur said. 'If you say so. But I can do without the hassle. If I've only got myself to please, there's no emotional conflict. And I like a quiet life, I'm afraid.'

'Oh, there's going to be someone out there, somewhere, who'll change your mind one of these days,' Mia said, 'you mark my words.' Her shrewd eyes narrowed slightly as she glanced over at Fleur, and she thought how fragile the girl looked—fragile and pale. She also seemed to have lost weight, which she could not afford to do.

Fleur turned, shrugging. 'We'll see,' she said lightly. There was a pause. 'As a matter of fact, I've not been very well lately, Mia. I've completely lost my appetite and I'm tired all the time. The doctor mentioned "stress"—how I hate that word—but I have agreed to take a longer than normal Christmas break, so I'm not due back to work until mid-January.'

'Well, why not stay on longer here, then?' Mia said at once. 'All the others are going back the day after Boxing Day, but I'm not returning to London until the second of January… We'll have some lovely extra time together. It'll do you good to be here in the peace and quiet, and Pat will love looking after you, spoiling you. And if her cooking can't bring your appetite back to life, no one's can. You've not made other plans, have you? Haven't got to go back to the parents for some TLC?'

'No, I haven't promised anything,' Fleur said quickly. 'I…haven't said anything to them about not feeling well lately… I don't want any fuss…'

'Well then, stay here and relax. Read. Walk. Watch telly. Stay in bed till mid-morning if you like. No one to please but yourself—that is what you want, isn't it?'

'Sounds wonderful,' Fleur said slowly, 'but I couldn't

outstay my welcome like that, Mia—I'd feel awful having someone to wait on me, prepare my meals…'

'I'm telling you—Pat will be ecstatic,' Mia assured her. 'It's a funny old life for her, really, looking after a big house that's got no one in it, sometimes for weeks on end.' She finished drying her hair and opened her wardrobe, peering inside. 'What to wear, what to wear,' she muttered to herself, before selecting jeans and a chunky woolen jumper. 'We must bring in all your stuff from the car,' she said over her shoulder, 'and then I'll leave you alone for an hour to settle in.' She smiled. 'It's going to be just the two of us until tomorrow evening, so we can have a good old gossipy natter.' She pulled her still damp hair free from the high neck of her jumper, and picked up her hairbrush. 'I only got home myself a couple of hours ago,' she added. 'Hasn't Pat made the tree look fantastic? That woman really is a treasure.'

'She doesn't live in all the time, then?' Fleur asked.

'Oh, no, only when one of us, or some friends, are here. She lives in one of the estate cottages with her mother, but the two of them make sure everything's OK while the house is unoccupied. My brother is regularly away, working for a law firm who engage him on a part-time basis—of course, he's the one in charge of the estate now that our parents aren't here any more.' Mia stopped brushing her hair for a second, biting her lip.

Fleur said quickly, 'It must be difficult for him, juggling work and the estate. I don't expect he thought he'd have to take over here quite so soon.'

'He certainly didn't. Neither of us did,' Mia said. 'For both our parents to die so unexpectedly, four years ago, before either of them had reached sixty, was a dreadful shock.'

'I know,' Fleur said sympathetically. She had never met Mia's parents, or her brother, but knew all about them from her friend.

'And it dropped Pengarroth Hall prematurely right into Seb's lap,' Mia said. 'He was only thirty, and enjoying his life in London—rather too much, in some people's opinion! But my playboy brother had to grow up some time—to the disappointment of the party crowd and his many lady friends. I don't think he was best pleased. Still—' she brightened up quickly, as Mia always did, whatever the circumstances '—he's got used to it. And it pleases Gran. She and Gramps loved Pengarroth Hall—where they lived too, of course, for most of their lives.'

'Goodness—is your grandmother still alive?' Fleur asked.

'You bet!' Mia said. 'And we both visit her often. As a matter of fact, I believe she was a bit of a girl-about-town in her youth, when she met my grandfather. And she still loves being in the big city, where she lives in the most amazing flat. She's in her mid-eighties now, but she's got a large circle of friends... They go to the theatre, out to meals, play bridge regularly. There's no stopping her. But she loves to think that Pengarroth Hall is still in the family. Worships Sebastian, of course. He's the golden boy.'

'She's not coming here for Christmas?' Fleur asked.

'We couldn't persuade her,' Mia replied. 'Especially when she knew there'd be a crowd of us in residence. Said she'd rather spend it with her own friends, and leave us to ours. She always spends a couple of months here in the summer, though.'

'She sounds a lot of fun,' Fleur said wistfully, thinking what a solitary sort of life she had led, with no siblings and never having known *her* grandparents, or any other family members.

'She's fantastic,' Mia said breezily. 'We love her to bits.'

Going downstairs to collect Fleur's belongings from the car, Mia stopped to pat the sleeping dog's head as they went by.

'Poor old Benson,' she said softly. 'He's so old now, snoozes most of the time, but Sebastian won't have another dog on the premises, not until Benson has popped his clogs. Says this is Benson's territory.' She rubbed the dog's nose with her forefinger. 'Anyway, Frank, our groundsman, has enough to do without having a young animal to train.'

Fleur made a face. 'I think I met Frank earlier,' she said, 'and was roundly told off for trespassing. I came in at the wrong gate—the upper one—by mistake.'

'Oh, you mad woman!' Mia said. 'But I'm a bit scatty with directions so that was probably my fault. Why—what did he say?'

'More or less told me to clear off and to be more observant in future and follow appropriate signs.'

Mia giggled. 'He can be a bossy boots and rather short-tempered,' she said, 'but he's worth his weight in gold. Seb relies on him totally when he's not here. And of course when visitors come to shoot game in the autumn, Frank runs everything.'

Later, when she was alone, Fleur unpacked and, taking the hint from her friend, changed into jeans and a green jumper that did marvelous things for her eyes and brushed her hair back into a ponytail. Then she wiped off all her make-up before moisturizing her skin. It felt so good not to have to bother about looking immaculate and put aside her heels for the evening. She suddenly felt upbeat, looking forward to a cosy evening with one of her best friends. Then, slipping her bare feet into her Uggs, she left the room and went downstairs, almost colliding with Pat at the bottom.

'Oh, there you are,' the woman said. 'Mia's just dashed down the road to deliver some Christmas presents. Go into the sitting room—the one there on the left. I'll bring you some tea in a few minutes.'

Fleur wandered along the hallway to the room which had been indicated, going straight over to the huge fireplace, where some logs were burning brightly in the grate. This holiday had all the elements of a real Dickensian Christmas, she thought, feeling thrilled all over again that she was a guest here. The large room was comfortably—though not opulently—furnished, with sofas and armchairs, none of which were new. The carpet, though worn, felt soft under her feet and she kicked off her Uggs as she sat down on the armchair nearest to the fire. Leaning her head back contentedly, she closed her eyes. She could get used to this, she thought dreamily, this serenity, this feeling of well-being. Perhaps—perhaps she *could* allow herself to be persuaded to take Mia up on the offer to stay on for a while longer…just so long as she was certain she wouldn't be in anyone's way. Perhaps for an extra week, she thought, wiggling her bare toes in front of the flames, a delightful drowsiness beginning to seep over her.

After a few moments, something made her open her eyes and with a start she found herself staring up into the familiar face she'd seen before today. The groundsman stood there, wearing well-cut jeans and dark polo shirt, one hand thrust casually into his pocket. He was obviously very much at home here, Fleur thought instinctively. She smiled faintly.

'Oh…hello,' she said non-committally, nestling back down into the chair. 'We meet again.' She hoped he would feel a slight pang of conscience when he remembered his curt behaviour earlier, especially when it was obvious that she was a guest.

His eyes narrowed slightly as he took in her appearance, noting the willowy figure and unblemished skin devoid of artifice, but, before he could say a word, Mia breezed into the room—stopping short as she saw him standing there.

'Seb! What on earth are *you* doing here?'

'I do live here from time to time, remember,' he said, going towards her and giving her a bear hug. 'Hi, Mia.'

'Yes—but you said you wouldn't be home until Christmas morning,' Mia protested. 'What made you change your mind?'

'It was changed for me—but I can't be bothered to explain,' he replied. 'Why—does it matter?'

'No, of course not. You just took me by surprise, that's all. And Pat didn't tell me, either.'

'Because she didn't know until half an hour ago. I didn't see her at lunch time when I arrived, and then I took myself off straight away to look around the estate while it was still light. It's Frank's day off today.' He paused. 'Still, I'm here now. Hope my presence hasn't ruined your plans too much.'

'Idiot,' Mia said fondly. 'Course not.' She went over to Fleur, whose colour had risen perceptibly, and who suddenly wanted to kick herself. This was not Frank the groundsman, this was Sebastian Conway! What a stupid assumption to have made!

'Have you two introduced yourselves?' Mia asked. 'Fleur—this is my gorgeous brother, and this, Sebastian, is one of my very best friends, Fleur Richardson.'

Fleur stood up then, slowly, wishing she could just disappear, but Sebastian came across and held out a strong hand, gripping hers firmly. He looked down at her, his thoughtful black eyes glinting in the firelight.

'We have met before, haven't we,' he murmured. Then, 'You really should have said who you were.'

Mia looked bewildered. 'What's going on?' she demanded.

Fleur looked at her helplessly. 'This was the man I thought was…Frank…' she began, and Mia burst out laughing.

'Oh, Seb! Fleur told me you were horrible to her, accusing her of trespassing! How could you?'

'If I'd known she was one of your guests, I would have said nothing, but escorted her back to her car and directed her to the house,' he said. 'It's just that Frank is very protective of all the new saplings—for which I'm grateful to him—and I was out checking up on them when we… er…Fleur and I…came across each other.'

'Well, allow me to apologize for my earlier misdemeanour.' Fleur smiled, trying to sound more relaxed than she felt at that precise moment.

'And I offer mine for running you off,' he said equably.

Just then, Pat came in with a tray of tea. She smiled as she set the things down on a low table. 'It's great to have folk about the place for a change,' she exclaimed, standing back and looking from one to another happily. 'Supper will be ready in forty-five minutes,' she added as she left.

As the three of them sat drinking their tea and chatting, Fleur was painfully aware of Sebastian's long legs stretched out in front of him, of his powerful frame and strong features. This was a man to be reckoned with, she thought.

A man used to getting his own way. A man who liked to be in control. Who would always *expect* to be in control.

And Sebastian, as he listened to his sister's high-spirited account of what she'd been up to since they'd last been together, was making judgements of his own. For once, this particular friend of Mia's—and he'd met a few—didn't fall into the normal category he'd come to expect. She wasn't lowering her eyes at him, or exhibiting the kind of come-on tactics that were all too familiar. She was undeniably very attractive—and, from her self-deprecating description of the research work she was engaged in, unusually clever. But she displayed an oddly distant attitude which he found disconcerting. She was not aloof exactly, but there was a wistful coolness about her that he confessed to finding distinctly intriguing. He stood up quickly and went across to the cabinet to pour some drinks.

CHAPTER TWO

'THAT really was the best Christmas I've ever, ever had,' Fleur said as she and Mia helped Pat to clear up in the kitchen. Pat, with assistance from Beryl, her mother, had produced the most amazing food all over the holiday, and now, with everyone else having just departed, it was time to wind down from the festivities.

'I don't think I'll want another thing to eat—not until tomorrow, anyway!' Mia joked. 'You really are fantastic, Pat—thank you *so* much for all your hard work. I'm still dribbling after that goose!'

'Well, you know I always look forward to you and Sebastian being home,' Pat said, spreading some tea towels to dry, 'and all your friends were very appreciative. No one left anything on their plates, anyway,' she added. 'Always a good sign.'

Mia glanced at Fleur, thinking how easily she had fitted in with everyone else, and how she'd seemed to enjoy all the festive food—despite her apparent lack of appetite.

'Yes, everyone enjoyed themselves thoroughly,' Mia said. 'We might do it all over again next year!' She giggled. 'Mandy's such a naughty girl, though, isn't she? She told me that she'd intended seducing Sebastian this time—she's tried before—hoping that the spirit of Christmas, or Christmas spirits, might make him fall for her charms.'

'Hmm, some hopes,' Pat snorted. 'Sebastian is much too clever for antics like that. And I don't blame him either.' Pat had known the family for too long not to feel quite comfortable about expressing her opinions. 'Especially in view of…you know…' Her voice trailed off.

'Yes, you're right, Pat. Poor old Seb…' Mia began, pulling out a chair to sit down.

'What's the matter with poor old Seb?' he demanded as he came into the kitchen.

'Oh, I was just saying how incorrigible Mandy is,' Mia said hurriedly. 'Flirting outrageously with all the guys—including you, Seb. Or didn't you even notice?'

Sebastian merely grinned at that, and Mia went on, 'Not that you showed your face much anyway; we hardly saw anything of you.'

It was true that he'd been rather conspicuous by his absence, Fleur thought as she glanced up at him briefly. He'd apparently spent Christmas Eve with friends in the area, not coming home until the small hours, but had joined them for the main Christmas Day meal and for supper again on Boxing Day. But he'd seemed to prefer leaving the eight of them to enjoy themselves without him—and Fleur couldn't blame him. They were all just that few years younger than him, and she'd noticed that sometimes their chatter and alcohol-fuelled banter had appeared to bore him. Her eyes narrowed briefly. He was sort of…mysterious…in a way, she thought. Certainly not your normal run-of-the-mill handsome bachelor. The only woman he seemed to have eyes for was his sister—who he clearly adored. But Fleur couldn't help wondering what he thought about *her*. She'd noticed him glance at her speculatively from time to time, but he didn't seem to like—or dislike—her. She was, after all, just another of his sister's friends, who he seemed to tolerate but, as Mia was entitled to invite whoever she wanted to, he'd have to put up with it.

By now, it was late afternoon and already darkening outside, and Fleur suddenly felt a need to get out into the open air. Although they'd all gone for short walks once or twice during the holiday—keeping strictly to the paths which Sebastian had recommended—most of the time had been spent eating, drinking, dozing, watching films and telling ghost stories.

'I'd love to go for a walk, Mia,' she said, looking down at her friend, who was lounging back in her chair lazily. 'Just for half an hour…can we?'

'Oh, Fleur…count me out!' Mia begged. 'Tramping about in soggy undergrowth is the last thing on *my* mind. But—hey, Seb will go with you—he'll protect you from all the wild animals out there. Won't you, Seb?'

Fleur felt a huge wave of embarrassment sweep over her. 'No! There's no need for that… It doesn't matter, really,' she said quickly. 'It's just me being silly. Forget it.'

'No need to forget it,' Sebastian said casually. 'But we must go now while there's still some light.' He glanced at her. He'd already observed her obvious stylish dress sense, and on Christmas evening, as they'd all sat around the candle-lit table, her simple black low-necked dress and the fine gold chain around her neck had, in his opinion, set her apart from everyone else. 'You'd better dress warmly—you brought some walking boots with you, I hope.'

Well, that sounded a bit headmasterly, Fleur thought, but still—presumably he had her best interests at heart. 'Oh, yes—Mia warned me that I'd need them,' she said. She went towards the door. 'I'll get a thicker sweater and a waterproof. Shan't be a minute.'

As soon as she'd gone, Mia said, 'Seb, I want you to do me a big, big favour—' and he interrupted.

'Not another one. What's it this time?'

'It's not for me, personally,' Mia replied. 'It's just that… well…Fleur is going to stay on for a bit—about ten days— after I've gone back. Pat has kindly agreed to look after her for me, so that's no problem…'

'It'll be a pleasure,' Pat said, as she finally emptied the dishwasher. 'I like your friend, Mia—she was always the first to offer to help us out.'

'What's it got to do with me?' Sebastian demanded.

'I want you to kind of…well…take her under your wing while she's here. You said you weren't going back to London until the end of the month, and…'

'What exactly does "taking her under my wing" involve?' Sebastian said resignedly.

'Oh, nothing much, you know…just be *nice*—be around to share the occasional meal with her, maybe show her the area, take her down to the pub…' She paused. 'I'm worried about her. She's lost weight since I last saw her, and I know she doesn't sleep too well. A bit of a holiday here will do her the world of good, but she will need some company now and again and you're just the man.'

'Now, look Mia…' Sebastian began.

She said at once, 'Oh, don't worry, Seb, it's not what *you're* thinking. I wouldn't dream of trying my hand at the matchmaking game. Never again. Not with you or anyone else. I've learned my lesson in *that* department.'

'I should think so too, and I'm very glad to hear it,' he

said flatly. It had been another "best friend" of his sister's—she seemed to have so many—who, not so long ago, he'd become engaged to, which had turned out to be a total disaster. And since then he'd hardly looked at another woman, no longer seeming to need female company. Not in any serious sense. And that worried him slightly.

'In any case,' Mia went on, 'Fleur is not on the market, so you can relax. She's not interested in tying herself down to any man, so you're quite safe. I guarantee it.' She sighed. 'I feel so sorry for her, that's all. Despite all her outward success and although ostensibly she's a free woman, she seems sort of…trapped…as if she can't break free to be really happy. It must be dreadful to feel like that.' Mia made a face as she thought about it.

'Well, I don't mind being civil, if that's what you mean,' Sebastian said shortly, 'but don't expect me to provide non-stop entertainment for her, will you? I've got four weeks to catch up on things here before I'm due back in London, and I've got appointments in Truro with the surveyor and the accountant…but…' he paused '…yes, all right, I'll arrange to be here for some of the time to hold your friend's hand—if that's what you want.'

Mia smiled up at him. 'You don't need to go *that* far,' she said demurely, 'and Fleur won't thank you for getting close enough to hold her hand, either. Just be your darling self and keep her company now and then, that's all I'm asking. You'll be just the tonic I think she needs.'

Fleur, about to go back into the kitchen, had paused outside the door just long enough to overhear most of what had been said…and she froze, horrified. The last thing in the world she wanted was to be a burden to anyone—certainly not to the somewhat austere Sebastian! How could Mia put

him—put them both—in such an awkward and embarrassing position? But what could be done about it now? She
could hardly burst in and tell them she'd heard his reluctant
reply to Mia's request—or even say that she'd changed her
mind and wasn't going to stay after all. What excuse could
she give? She'd already accepted the invitation, and Pat had
been so touchingly pleased. Fleur bit her lip, feeling her
cheeks flood with colour as she stood there. It was obvious
that Sebastian saw her as an unwelcome intrusion into his
busy life, and that was the last thing she'd envisaged when
she'd accepted Mia's suggestion. Then common sense prevailed, and she took a deep breath. There was a simple way
out of this, she thought. She'd stay a day or two after Mia
had gone before inventing a telephone call telling her to
return early. It could be about something important in the
lab that needed her input. That was it—no need to panic,
after all, she told herself.

She opened the door and went inside, and Sebastian
clicked his fingers for the dog to get up from the floor.

'We'll take Benson with us,' he said, 'as we shan't be
going too far. A short walk won't tire him too much.'

Outside, it was much colder than Fleur had thought, and
she turned up the collar of her jacket. Sebastian glanced
down at her briefly.

'We can always go back if you find you're not enjoying
this,' he said casually.

'No, it's fine. I'd like to walk,' Fleur said, not looking
at him. 'But…I'm perfectly all right by myself if you've
things to do. I know this path because we all walked this
way yesterday, and Benson will keep me company.'

'Oh, Mia would kill me if I abandoned you,' he said.

They walked in silence for a few minutes and, although

it was certainly wet and soggy—as Mia had predicted— there was something magical about their surroundings...the magic Fleur had felt when she'd arrived at the beginning of her stay, and it made her say suddenly, 'It must be wonderful to be able to wander in these enchanted woods whenever you want to...' She hesitated. 'Mia told me that you work part-time in London, but...how often do you get down here? You must hate having to go back to town.'

He thought about that for a moment. Then, 'Sometimes I do,' he admitted, 'but, in any case, the time is coming when I shall have to part company with the firm I work for and live here permanently. It's getting more and more difficult to stretch myself between the two places.'

Something in his tone of voice made Fleur look up quickly. 'Will you mind that?' she asked quietly.

'I'm getting used to the idea,' he said. 'Of course, I knew it would come to an end one day, but I never expected it to happen quite so soon.' He paused. 'I've made a lot of friends in London that, with the best will in the world, I'll eventually lose touch with. It's inevitable. I'll be well and truly buried down here for keeps. I've just got to accept it.'

Neither of them spoke for a few moments. 'It's very annoying—to say the least—when your life is planned out for you,' Fleur began, and he interrupted.

'You sound as if you speak from experience,' he said, and she smiled up at him quickly.

'Well, in a way I do,' she said. 'Not that *I* have been given the responsibility of having to hold the reins of a large family estate, nothing like that, but...'

'Go on,' he said, wanting to know more.

'It's just that, well, I had my own plans for what I wanted to do with my life but my father had other ideas.' She paused.

'He persuaded me…' she didn't utter the more truthful word *insisted* '…that my true vocation was in the sciences, and that with my "exceptional brain"—his words, not mine—I had a duty to use it for the good of others. So that's why I'm in medical research.' She shook her head briefly. 'I enjoy the work—of course I do—it's fulfilling and very exciting when we make any sort of breakthrough. But such a lot of it is painstaking and repetitive and often very disappointing.' She looked up at him again. 'So there you are—that's my life sorted out for me. And I had such ideas of my own. Probably ridiculous when I really think about it.'

He grinned back at her and for the first time Fleur saw his heart-stopping smile, a smile enlivened by immaculate, strong white teeth. 'Go on—I'm waiting for the punchline,' he said.

Fleur sighed, looking away. 'I always imagined myself as an opera singer,' she said, almost apologetically. 'I realize that it was probably an impossible dream—the professional stage is overwhelmingly competitive, and luck is such a huge factor. But it would have been good to at least have tried.' She gave a short laugh. 'Not that luck is *my* second name—I mean, I never win *anything*, never win raffles or anything that relies on chance. Some people win things all the time.'

'Yes, they do,' he agreed. 'Actually, I do win things now and then.' He didn't bother to add that in the circles he mixed in he was constantly asked to purchase massively priced tickets for good causes and that he always obliged, very generously. Which probably increased his chances. 'But do go on,' he said. 'You've obviously had musical training?'

'Oh, yes—I *was* allowed that,' Fleur said, a slight trace of bitterness in her tone. 'I achieved all my grades up to the point where I should have gone on to gain higher qualifications…then the paternal foot was well and truly put down. So—' she sighed '—as you so rightly said, it's hard to do two things at once. In my case, impossible.' She shrugged. 'So I content myself with enjoying music at a distance, as a listener and a devoted member of numerous audiences. And singing along with my CDs. When I was still living at home, that was how I learned all the famous arias, making sure that my father was never around when I was doing it. He would *not* have approved!'

The tangible note of regret in her voice made Sebastian's brow crease slightly. That didn't sound fair, he thought. 'Well, in a way, our situations are not dissimilar,' he said. 'We've both ended up doing what others have decided we should. Although—' he smiled down at her again '—in my case it was the hand of fate that merely hastened my inevitable destiny.' He hesitated. 'But it's not too late for you, is it? You could change the course of things, couldn't you?'

Fleur chuckled. 'My father would *never* forgive me if I did that,' she exclaimed. 'And he would make me feel so guilty if I gave up my career to pursue such a dramatically different path. Which, in his view, would be a very flippant one. I mean, you don't save lives by singing songs, do you? He has no time for music and rarely listens to any. But my mother does—though she doesn't often play the piano any more because it disturbs my father when he's working.' She shook her head. 'No, it is much too late for me now, Sebastian.'

With a little jolt of surprise, Fleur realized that that was the first time she had called him by name…but the easy conversation had seemed to put them on a more comfortable footing.

By this time they'd walked on quite a bit further than Sebastian had intended, and he glanced at the dog, who was padding rather forlornly behind them.

'I think we ought to go back now,' he said. 'Benson's had enough and we shan't be able to see a thing in a minute, though I did bring my torch.'

Fleur smiled up at him. 'We don't want to tire Benson out, but I could carry on like this for hours!'

Yes, I believe she could, Sebastian thought. Even though she was obviously more used to being in town, Fleur had a definite affinity with the countryside, had picked her own way over the pits, humps and bumps of the terrain without any help from him. He hadn't once felt the need to put his hand under her elbow, or steady her as they'd made their way. Perhaps she wasn't as fragile as she looked.

When she knew that their walk was coming to an end, Fleur made a sudden decision—thanks to the rather unexpected familiarity which seemed to have developed between them. Keeping her eyes fixed firmly ahead, she said lightly, 'By the way, Sebastian, you needn't worry that I'm going to get in the way of your plans while I'm here.' She hesitated. 'And I'm…sorry…that Mia has put you in the unenviable position of being my "minder". But I assure you that I am very used to looking out for myself. I do it all the time, because I live alone.' Now she did look up to find his searching eyes—black and intense and clearly visible, even in the gloom—staring right into hers. 'It was wrong of Mia to expect anything from you where I'm concerned—anything at all—I certainly don't. It's extremely kind of you—of both of you—to invite me to stay, and I don't anticipate being bored. I can never remember being bored, in any situation,' she added. She smiled. 'I shall explore the area thoroughly, and lock it all into my memory so that when I get home I can relive it. And you must just…just pretend that I'm not here.'

Sebastian was ready to admit that it would be hard to follow *that* instruction! Fleur Richardson was the first woman for a very long time to excite his interest. But, although it was patently clear that the conversation with his sister had been overheard, it didn't worry him in the least. He was seldom embarrassed or fazed by anything any more.

'Isn't there a man at home who'll be gasping for your return?' he asked bluntly.

Fleur smiled at that. 'No,' she said simply. 'No, there isn't.'

His rather peremptory enquiry made Fleur feel that she could ask a similar question. What was sauce for the goose…

'And you?' she asked coolly. 'Don't you have a lady ready to be mistress of Pengarroth Hall?'

'Don't bother to ask,' he replied, his mouth tightening at the thought.

Just before they stepped into the pool of light shining from the house, they both automatically slowed in their tracks, as if neither of them wanted to bring this particular time to an end, and standing closer to her now, closer than he had during their walk, Sebastian looked down at her.

'I do have things to do during January,' he said, 'but I'm also due for some time off. So…as Mia has told me I must, it will give me great pleasure to spend some of it with you. And, because I always obey my sister's wishes, I will take you under my wing—and you must try and enjoy it. Because,' he said patiently, 'that's what Mia wants us to do.' He smiled down at her then, a crooked, knowing smile that made Fleur's knees tremble slightly.

Well, he seemed to have cleared the air without any difficulty, Fleur thought, feeling strangely relieved. He obviously believed in coming straight to the point in any situation. But, whatever he said, she'd make herself scarce most of the time she was at Pengarroth Hall. There was certainly no need for him to add *her* name to his list of commitments!

CHAPTER THREE

MIA lay quite still, watching Fleur's sleeping form in the bed opposite her. Frowning momentarily, Mia wondered how her friend would really manage to enjoy herself when she, Mia, had returned to London. It would naturally feel very different at Pengarroth Hall without her, Mia realized, and although Sebastian had said he'd 'look after' Fleur—as much as his work would allow—would that be enough to keep her happily occupied? Not to mention the fact that Seb could be an unknown quantity at times.

As if she knew she was being watched, Fleur suddenly opened her eyes and smiled, turning to lie on her back and stretching her arms above her head. 'Morning,' she said sleepily.

'D'you know what the time is?' Mia enquired and, without waiting for a reply, added, 'It's gone ten-thirty.' But she was genuinely pleased that Fleur seemed so much more relaxed and was definitely sleeping better than when she'd first arrived.

Fleur sat up then, hugging her knees. 'Well, we were very late to bed, weren't we?' she said, yawning. 'I've never spent New Year's Eve in a country pub before, with everyone so friendly and singing along…' She paused. 'You and Sebastian knew almost everyone there.'

'Quite a few,' Mia agreed. 'Like us, some return home for holidays and the festive season, so we meet up then. But it's all very uncomplicated and informal.'

'I thought it was great,' Fleur said appreciatively, 'and I've never been kissed by so many complete strangers in my life when the twelve o'clock chimes rang out!' She didn't bother to mention that Sebastian hadn't joined in with that part of the proceedings—not that *she* could see, anyway—he certainly had not kissed *her*! But, even in that large, milling crowd, he had stood head and shoulders above most of them and had looked very debonair, casually dressed, his black hair sleek and shining with health.

'Oh, that only happens on this one night of the year,' Mia said, 'when everyone goes a bit crazy. I wouldn't like you to have the wrong impression of our neighbours, or our lifestyles!' She threw back her duvet and went across to the window, drawing back the curtains. 'Oh, look—there's been a really heavy frost again…everything looks so pretty.' She paused. 'And there's my brother, with Benson.' She yawned loudly. 'Seb's always up and about at the crack of dawn—I wonder if he ever goes to bed at all.'

'You and Sebastian are very close, aren't you,' Fleur said enviously. 'I wish *I'd* had a brother—or a sister.'

'Hmm,' Mia said. 'Seb and I have always got on brilliantly, it's true, but I think the age gap between us sometimes makes him feel responsible for me. Too responsible. He has played the heavy-handed head of the house once or twice—which can be extremely annoying—and with which I am not well pleased, I can tell you.'

'Oh?' Fleur said, not altogether surprised. Even though

Sebastian seemed very tolerant and affectionate towards Mia, she could imagine him playing the dominant male when he felt like it. 'Why—what happened?'

'Oh, it was over relationships, of course…I used to feel he was vetting my boyfriends all the time, but the big crunch came over Andrew… You remember Andy? You met him once or twice, didn't you… About four years ago, it was.'

'I did,' Fleur said at once. 'He was a real charmer, and I thought he was the one for you. I was staggered when that all fell apart.'

'Yes, well, it fell apart because my big brother found things out about him and confronted him about it…in my flat! It was the most embarrassing, hurtful night of my life!' She shuddered. 'In Seb's defence, he *had* tried several times to warn me, privately, but of course I wouldn't hear a word against Andy. Wouldn't believe it. So in the end the whole wretched business was brought right into my sitting room! And Andy couldn't deny any of it! I thought I was going to die at the time, but of course I didn't,' she added cheerfully.

'Another woman?' Fleur said, curiosity overcoming her normal reluctance to pry into other people's affairs.

'Oh, nothing as simple as *that*,' Mia said, reaching for her dressing gown. 'No, it turned out that Andy was engaged in financial skullduggery—big time. Sebastian had obviously decided to make some enquiries, and he dug out some real dirt, I can tell you. And I was as mad as hell that my brother had interfered in my life… I felt I should be allowed to make my own mistakes. But, of course, every single thing he'd found out about Andy proved to be true— and if I'd had my own way I might be visiting my husband in jail by now!' She grimaced. 'I am grateful to Seb—but

I didn't see it quite like that at the time.' She turned to look at Fleur. 'And the last remark Andy made to me was that he'd make damned sure his next woman didn't have a hard-nosed, interfering lawyer for a brother!'

'Where's Andrew now?' Fleur wanted to know.

'Oh, disappeared to Spain or somewhere, I believe…no doubt carrying on his nefarious exercises undetected—for the moment. Seb never took it further—as he said, he's not a member of the police force. All he wanted was Andrew out of my life. And in that he was very successful indeed!'

Even though it had clearly been very fortunate for Mia that her boyfriend's activities had been exposed before it was too late, Fleur could readily understand how her friend would have felt. And it confirmed Fleur's impression of Sebastian. A force to be reckoned with and a force not easily deterred. Like someone else she knew!

'I am going to be very jealous thinking of you here, just lazing around,' Mia said, changing the subject. 'Though I do hope the days won't drag for you, Fleur.'

Fleur got out of bed as well then, and went across to join Mia. 'Don't give that a thought,' she said. 'I'm never bored. It'll be wonderful to just let each day take care of itself instead of trying to make every hour count.' She paused. 'The only thing is, I didn't bring enough clothes with me for an extended stay… I'll probably have to do some washing.'

'That shouldn't be a problem, and I know we're not the same size—or shape,' Mia said quickly, 'but help yourself to anything of mine, Fleur… Well, you'll be all right for skirts if my jeans don't fit. And sweaters galore, which remain here permanently. Anyway,' she added, 'no one dresses up down here. Just be warm and comfortable and forget about looking good. Not that you wouldn't look good, even in sackcloth and ashes!' She turned away. 'You go and shower first,' she said, flopping back down on her bed. 'Take your time—I told Pat we'd get our own breakfast and lunch today so that she could go home to her cottage for a few hours.' She smiled. 'And that's another thing I'll be picturing—you sitting down to Pat's glorious meals.'

'She's certainly a fantastic cook,' Fleur said. 'I shall be twice the size by the time I go home.'

'Hmm,' Mia said, thinking that even if she was, Fleur wouldn't ever reach *her* weight. But she was really pleased to see how relaxed she had become over the days. She looked less wan and more like the enthusiastic young woman she'd always been at school and university.

Neither of them spoke for a few moments as Fleur remained by the window, gazing out at the gardens below, her eyes searching the near and far distance...but Sebastian had gone.

The following morning, after Mia had left Pengarroth Hall, Fleur decided to explore the area outside the house and grounds. She had not yet seen anything like the full extent of the estate, but felt it would be a good move to go somewhere different today. She didn't want to keep bumping into Sebastian—whom she and Mia had seen very little of since New Year's Eve. He'd looked in on them briefly last evening, but hadn't joined them for supper. It was obvious that he was very preoccupied, and Fleur had seen him and Frank in the distance once or twice, clearly in deep discussion.

Fleur had persuaded Pat that she could easily manage to get her own breakfast and lunch every day, and that at most she need only concern herself with the day's main meal...and that was more for Sebastian's sake than her own.

'We'll see about that,' Pat had said 'I shall be popping in and out, in any case, but it'll be useful to be with Mum a bit, because she's not too well at the moment. She's going to be eighty-five this year,' she added, 'so it's only to be expected if she has an off day sometimes.'

It was a clear, icy morning as Fleur set off along the winding drive, well wrapped up against the cold as Mia had instructed her, admitting to herself again that she hadn't felt as good and as energetic as this for ages. She also had to admit that she'd scarcely thought about work—or her parents—for the entire holiday. A change of scene, especially with Mia there, was what she'd obviously been needing after all, she thought, not those tablets the doctor had prescribed. Then she put her hand to her mouth, suddenly realizing she'd forgotten to take any for the last two days. Oh, well, she'd take one tomorrow.

Outside the huge gate, she stopped for a moment, wondering whether to go up the hill or down to the valley—the direction in which Sebastian had driven them to the pub the other night. Downhill sounded the better option, she thought, turning decisively and starting to make her way along the narrow, high-hedged road.

She'd hardly gone any distance when she heard a car approaching rapidly behind her and she instinctively stood back, well into the side. It wasn't a car—it was a Land Rover, with Sebastian at the wheel, and he immediately pulled up and spoke through the open window.

'Good morning. Want a lift? Do you know where you're going?' he asked.

Fleur smiled faintly—this was just what she was trying to avoid. 'No—on both counts, thanks,' she said. 'I'm just going to have a look around, sort of get my bearings.' She paused, conscious that he was staring unashamedly at her, right into her eyes, burrowing his way into her soul! She hoped he approved of the thick jacket of Mia's that she was wearing, with its fur-lined hood framing her face. But his expression remained as it always was—curiously unfathomable—and it had its usual effect so that she quickly tore her gaze away. 'What's at the bottom of this hill?' she asked, pointing ahead.

'Well, when you get there—and it's more than a mile—there are some houses, cottages, a couple of farms, a few shops, the village hall and the pub. Which you've already been in,' he said. 'Plus the river, of course—which is in full flood at the moment.' He paused. 'Why don't you hop in—I can at least give you a ride one way.'

Fleur hesitated, then, 'Oh, go on, then,' she said, slightly reluctantly. Her plan had been to give him a wide berth today, to keep clear of Pengarroth Hall and not be under his feet, but thanks to him, that plan had come unstuck straight away.

He leaned across and opened the passenger door, stretching out his hand to pull her up as she climbed aboard. His firm grasp enveloped her hand and she slammed the door quickly behind her, not looking across at him as he revved the engine. They set off down the hill at considerable speed and after a moment Fleur did turn her head. He was wearing heavy-duty gear, as before, she noted, though the sturdy fabric of his trousers couldn't disguise the strength of his firm thighs. But his hands, brown and lean as he held the steering wheel, were surprisingly smooth, the fingers long and sensitive. Which was hardly surprising, Fleur thought, because although today he could be mistaken for a farmer, he was a businessman, a lawyer. A man of many parts, and of obvious distinction. She sighed briefly. Why was she dissecting him like this? she asked herself. He was just another male person, the sort she came across all the time. But…no…that wasn't true, she acknowledged. She couldn't remember ever having been in the company of someone so outstandingly handsome, so out-of-your-mind gorgeous. The fact that he had an undoubtedly imperious streak was a bit of a turn-off— she remembered their first encounter!—and yet, who could blame him? He had a lot of responsibilities, both here and in London. A weak-minded individual wouldn't get very far. But he was obviously capable of other, much more likeable qualities—proved by his affection and care for Mia. On balance, Fleur thought wryly, she'd be very happy to have him for a brother.

'You're quiet,' he observed non-committally. 'Are you feeling OK?'

Fleur looked at him sharply. 'Why do you ask? I'm fine, thank you.'

'Oh, it was only that Mia hinted you'd been off colour lately, that's all. Though you look good to me,' he added, smiling briefly across at her.

Oh, Mia, really! Fleur thought. She didn't want her health discussed—certainly not with Sebastian. He probably thought he'd have to be on standby to ring the doctor in the middle of the night if she had a funny turn! She gave a short unnecessary cough. 'I've been suffering from a slight case of over-work, that's all,' she said lightly. 'This time away is already working wonders—plus Pat's wonderful meals, of course. So there's no need for you…for *anyone*…to worry about me.'

'I wasn't worried,' he said casually.

'That's all right, then,' she replied.

They reached the bottom of the hill and he pulled up and drew into the side of the road. 'I'm seeing someone at this farm here, for an hour,' he said, and Fleur shrugged inwardly. He didn't have to explain his whereabouts to her. 'There are plenty of good walks around for you to try,' he went on, 'and there are the shops, over there—though I think your money's safe enough!' He paused. 'If you find your way down to the river, be careful. It's very wet, and it'll be muddy. I don't want to have to come and fish you out.'

Fleur opened the door and got out, slamming it shut. 'I'll be fine,' she said. 'Thanks for the lift.'

She stood back as he drove off, and she watched him take a sharp turn left and disappear up a farm track.

She started walking along slowly, revelling in her sur-roundings and the almost traffic free road, and comparing it all with manic London and the frantically busy hospital she worked at. But could anyone be really happy here, all the time? she wondered. She remembered Sebastian's words, and his obvious regret that soon he would have to give up practising law, cut off that part of his life, presum-ably for ever. It was bound to be hard for him at first, she thought. Then she shrugged. Why was she concerned about him? They were his problems, not hers.

After strolling around for about an hour, Fleur's steps automatically took her along the public footpath towards the river. She could hear it before she saw it and, when she did, Sebastian had been right. It was brimful, and gurgling along happily. As if to complete the picture, a watery sun suddenly broke through the clouds, slanting its rays through the trees, and Fleur stopped. What a great picnic spot this must be in the summer. Yet did the locals ever really appreciate what was on their doorstep? she wondered.

She began treading carefully along the undulating path, her eyes riveted to the magnetic sight of the water bubbling along beside her, when, without any warning at all, and as if by an unseen force, both her feet shot from beneath her on the slimy undergrowth and she landed full-length with a thud, ending with a slithery slide, her hands flailing helplessly about as they tried to find something to hold on to.

She lay there for a few seconds, wondering how she was going to get up. She'd have to be careful—everywhere around her was wet and there was plenty of potential for further disaster—though thankfully she was well away from the water's edge.

She saw that she was generously smeared with mud, which she foolishly transferred to her face as she wiped her now running nose with the back of her hand, and she groaned. Whatever must she look like? Staring down at herself helplessly, she saw that Mia's jacket was plastered all down one side, and on the front, and she knew that somehow she must get back to Pengarroth Hall before anyone saw her. And, to achieve that, there was that long trek back up the hill first…

Gingerly, she moved on to her side and grasped a convenient piece of log, which allowed her some support as she got to her feet, very relieved that she didn't seem to have hurt herself. The only thing hurt was her pride! What an idiotic thing to have happened, she scolded herself crossly—and she had nothing with her to try and repair the damage, either. She'd only come with a couple of tissues and a ten pound note in her pocket, which were no help at all. It was very unlike her not to be better equipped—she usually never went *anywhere* without her precious handbag, which always contained all the essentials. In fact, without it she almost felt undressed.

Now, she turned and began climbing upwards on to a higher path away from the water, her eyes intent on watching where she was treading, when Sebastian's deep voice made her look up quickly. He stood a few feet away, his hands in his pockets, the merest semblance of that crooked smile playing lightly on his lips.

'Oh…dear *me*…' was all he said, as he looked her up and down, and Fleur gritted her teeth, feeling overwhelmingly awkward. As she climbed closer to him, he put out a hand to pull her up beside him, and as he did they came perilously close to a bear hug! He held her to him for a few seconds before releasing her and staring at her from head to foot, as if lazily assessing the damage.

'You obviously took a little tumble,' he said, and Fleur's eyes narrowed slightly. The man was laughing at her, she thought, irritated.

'Well observed,' she said coolly. 'But I avoided a swim.'

'You're not hurt…?' he asked, and now the dark eyes were serious, the hint of amusement no longer there.

'Absolutely not. I'm fine. If a little sticky,' she replied, flapping her hands together and making it worse.

'Well, then, let's get you cleaned up,' he said purposefully, in a way which left no room for argument. 'They'll sort you out at the Black Horse.'

'Oh, but I'd better go home…I mean, back to Pengarroth Hall…' Fleur began. 'I thought…'

'And *I* thought we might as well have some lunch at the pub first,' he interrupted. 'They do good food—I know you enjoyed New Year's Eve, didn't you?' He glanced down at her again, and suddenly his heart missed a beat—or two! Although her somewhat crestfallen face was liberally smeared with mud, it did nothing to detract from her overt desirability—a characteristic he'd tried to dismiss since the very first moment he'd seen her….. and Sebastian Conway almost stopped in his tracks. *What* was that word which had slipped, almost unnoticed, into his stream of consciousness? *Desire?* That had disappeared, along with Davina's departure, a long time ago. Had this small, unassuming, mud-smeared woman, dressed in unglamorous winter wear, woken up his libido? He swallowed, a surge of pleasure—or was it relief that he wasn't dead after all?—coursing through him, and he looked away from her. Because if she gazed at him once more, with those beautiful, expressive sad eyes, he wouldn't be responsible for his actions!

He walked slightly away from her as they reached the lane, and he cleared his throat. 'I do think that a glass of wine and a spot of lunch will do you good, Fleur. The slightest fall can be a shock to the system. And, anyway, I'm hungry,' he added.

Fleur didn't bother to reply. He'd decided that they were going to eat at the pub, and that was what would happen, even though she would have much preferred to go back to Pengarroth Hall. But still, on reflection, it would get lunch out of the way, she thought. Pat was not coming back until it was time to prepare the evening meal, so she might just as well fall in with his wishes and eat here, now.

As soon as they set foot inside the pub, Joy, the landlady, took one look at Fleur and sized up the situation at once. 'Oh, my good lor',' she said in her lilting Cornish way. 'Just look at you!'

Fleur smiled apologetically. 'I was taking a walk—or rather a slide—by the river,' she began.

Sebastian cut in. 'Fleur would appreciate the use of your toilet facilities to get cleaned up, Joy,' he said, 'and then I think we'd like some lunch, please, plus a good bottle of red.'

There were, as yet, only a few customers drinking at the bar, and the woman beckoned to Fleur to follow her. 'I'll get you a decent towel, dear,' she said. 'There are only paper ones in there.' She smiled at Sebastian, handing him a menu. 'And you can be looking at this, Sebastian.'

Alone, Fleur sighed briefly. *Why* did she have to fall down and make such a fool of herself? She took off the jacket, examining it closely. All that mud would hopefully brush off when it was dry, she thought, putting it over the back of a chair for a moment, and noting that her jeans were relatively unscathed. She stared at her reflection in the rather dingy mirror and groaned. She had nothing with her to restore some of her confidence—no blusher, no lipstick, not even a comb to run through her hair, which she'd left loose that morning.

Sitting at a table by the roaring log fire in the bar, Sebastian half-stood as Fleur came back to join him, and he pulled out a chair for her. 'You look better,' he said casually. Then, 'Are you really sure there was no physical damage, Fleur?'

She smiled up at him quickly, shaking her head. 'Quite sure, thanks,' she replied.

While he'd been supposedly studying the menu, Sebastian's thoughts had been more occupied with what *could* have happened to Fleur, down there by herself. She could have badly sprained—or even broken—an ankle, and been lying there for goodness knew how long if he hadn't decided to try and find her. And it had only been a last-minute thought as he'd left the farm that had prompted him to check whether she was still around. He shuddered slightly, reminding himself that he'd actually not intended to go back to the house until much later on—so, if Fleur hadn't returned, it could easily have been dark before anyone had realized she was missing.

He'd handed her the menu and, after studying it for a moment, she gave it back and looked up at him, properly. 'I'm really sorry if I've…interrupted…your day,' she murmured.

Her bewitchingly long eyelashes were still wet from washing her face, and he noticed again the way she had of sometimes blinking in a kind of slow motion…which he admitted to finding strangely titillating. At this moment, she was totally unadorned, he thought, her face rather pale and her unusually untidy, loosely flowing, wavy hair touching her shoulders.

'You're not interrupting anything,' he lied. 'Stop worrying. And I've ordered red wine because I've noticed that's what you seem to prefer…'

Fleur couldn't help feeling surprised at the remark. She wouldn't have thought he cared enough about her—or any of Mia's friends—to be that observant. She bent forward slightly to warm her hands by the fire. 'I don't ever drink at lunch time,' she said, 'but I could be persuaded to make an exception—under certain circumstances. Thank you, Sebastian. Just one glass will be perfect.'

He grinned at her now, and she was aware again of his startlingly white teeth, which seemed to light up his rather serious bronzed features. 'And, as I'm driving, I'd better follow suit.' He paused. 'Joy will keep the bottle safe for us. We'll finish it another time.'

Fleur was about to say—*Look, there doesn't have to be another time—you don't have to do this, Sebastian. I'm all right by myself*...but she didn't. Because after that first stab of embarrassment when he'd turned up by the river, she'd been grateful of his presence and his company.

Suddenly, he bent forward too and took one of her hands in his, looking down intently. 'Look, you *have* hurt yourself, Fleur,' he said, almost accusingly. 'See—there's quite a bad graze here on your knuckles... Didn't you see it, feel it?'

'A bit,' Fleur conceded. 'But it's nothing, Sebastian, really. No blood. So, no blood, no tears. My father's maxim all my life.'

He said nothing, but didn't let go of her hand, gently tracing the affected part with his forefinger, and Fleur couldn't help liking the sensation it gave her!

Just then, Joy appeared with the wine, and she glanced down, her quick eyes taking in the scene. Sebastian Conway had not had a woman with him for far too long, in her opinion. And this one was obviously someone special. Even with all the hubbub on New Year's Eve she'd noticed her amongst Mia's crowd. And she'd also noticed Sebastian's eyes following her every move. Well, about time, the woman thought.

CHAPTER FOUR

'THIS is always the worst bit of Christmas,' Pat said, from her lofty position on top of the stepladder as she handed down the last of the decorations to Fleur.

'Yes, it is rather sad—the ending of something you've really enjoyed,' Fleur agreed, kneeling down to coil all the fairy lights into a large box. 'But time goes by so quickly, it'll soon be happening all over again.'

Just then, Sebastian came in and glanced at the two women. 'Hi there,' he said briefly. Then, 'Good—putting all the junk away and getting back to normality.'

'Oh *you*, Sebastian!' Pat exclaimed. 'Talk about not being in the spirit of the season!'

Still intent on her task, Fleur glanced quickly up at Sebastian and their eyes met for the fleetest of seconds. He was dressed, as usual, in outdoor gear, and his hair was tousled and wet from the early morning rain.

'I could murder a black coffee,' he said. 'Can I get us all some?'

'No, you cannot,' Pat said firmly, as she climbed carefully down from the ladder. 'I'll do that, Sebastian, if you'll be so kind as to take this tree outside.'

'My pleasure,' he said at once, as Pat left the room.

Fleur finished putting the lights away, then closed the box carefully and got to her feet.

Sebastian said, 'How've you been doing, Fleur, over the last few days?' He was feeling somewhat guilty because he'd seen hardly anything of her since her fall, not only because he'd had to be elsewhere, but because he was determined to avoid—as much as he could—any emotional entanglements, and he was honest enough to admit that Fleur could, if only she knew it, change his mind on the matter. When they'd sat together in the pub the other lunch time, two whole hours had passed like five minutes… He'd found her an engaging conversationalist, unpretentious without being coy, and with firm opinions which, though freely expressed, were never combative. And, as she'd become thoroughly relaxed in front of the fire, her face had glowed, enlivened by her eyes glistening in the light from the flickering flames. At the point when he'd reached for her hand and held it for those few moments—ostensibly to make sure she wasn't really hurt—a sudden warmth had coursed through *him*, too. But with that sensation had come a wariness of being entrapped again. Easier to start than to stop, he'd reminded himself cynically. Hadn't he always considered himself an astute judge of human nature—didn't his profession hang on that premise?

So how could he possibly have been blinded to the essential components of Davina's nature? He'd learned the truth eventually—fortunately before he'd made her his wife. But it had been a close run thing, the possibility of their union becoming the subject of much discussion, both at work and down here. The news of their split had travelled fast too, and his independent, rather private nature had resented the publicity bitterly. Not that all the facts of the debacle had ever generally been known, which was somehow worse because what people didn't know they made up. And the locals who'd been expecting a glitzy wedding to talk about had had to go away empty-handed. The lesson, for him, had been a hard one, and there would never be a next time. That much he'd promised himself.

Besides, was there a twenty-first century woman alive who'd be prepared to incarcerate herself down here in the wet Cornish countryside for the rest of her life? He very much doubted that! Today's women were different. They didn't want to be tied to someone else's expectations and demands. It might work for the first few months, or a year, but after that the novelty would soon wear off. No, he had set his singular course straight ahead, with no distracting turnings. Here, pretty much alone, was where he was to spend his days. And he knew that that was the best possible thing for him, and for Pengarroth Hall. It would have to be a child of Mia's who, eventually, took charge of the estate. Even if the name died out, the blood line would almost certainly continue.

'Oh, I've been having a great time, thanks,' Fleur replied cheerfully, in answer to his question. 'I've had the chance to really explore the area, and I've finally stopped getting lost every time I leave Pengarroth Hall. All the locals are so friendly…they love to stop for a chat. I feel as though I'm becoming part of the scenery!'

'Hmm,' Sebastian said briefly. No doubt tongues were beginning to wag already, he thought. He'd been aware of the landlady at the Black Horse darting them knowing glances from time to time. He cleared his throat. 'I'm sorry I haven't been around for a while,' he said, 'but I knew I was going to be caught up…'

'Please—there's no need to apologize,' Fleur said quickly, 'and…'

'No, perhaps not,' he said, 'but I did promise Mia that I'd be able to sort of…'

'You shouldn't have promised Mia *anything*—and she shouldn't have asked!' Fleur said, her colour rising, and angry again that Mia had taken it upon herself to interfere. Perhaps now was the time to invent that phone call, she thought, and go back home. 'If I'd thought,' she went on more calmly, 'that you—or anyone—were going to feel responsible for me, I'd have refused the invitation in the first place. I told you, I'm used to being alone, and I like it! I *like* doing my own thing without the constraints of having to fall in with other people's wishes.' She paused, looking up at him, her face flushed. 'Please—for heaven's sake— pretend I'm not here!'

He half-smiled as he looked down at her, resisting the temptation to cup her chin in his hands and place his lips on hers. How could he—or anyone—pretend this woman wasn't here? Even Pat, who had been known to show her disapproval of one or two of Mia's friends, seemed to genuinely like Fleur.

'OK,' he said easily, 'but first, you can guide this tree outside for me… We'll have to use the side door to the garden. Here, put these on.' He handed her his gloves, then went across and with surprisingly little effort heaved the tree out of its pot and leaned it towards Fleur, who immediately took it by a bough near the top and helped him guide it out of the hall, appreciating the gloves which protected her hands from the prickly pine needles.

'Coffee's ready,' Pat called out and, after they'd deposited the tree outside, Fleur and Sebastian joined her in the kitchen. Benson was stretched out in front of the warm stove and Fleur automatically bent down to pet him.

'I suppose Benson's tired from his walk?' she said, glancing up at Sebastian.

'No, because he hasn't had one yet,' Sebastian replied. 'I couldn't persuade him to accompany me earlier. And I'm seeing Frank up at the top end of the estate this morning, so this lazy dog will have to wait until later on for his stroll.'

'Oh, can I take him?' Fleur asked eagerly. 'I know the places we're allowed to go. Will he come with me?...I haven't been out myself yet, anyway.'

'I'm sure he'd love to go with you,' Sebastian replied, taking his mug of coffee from Pat.

The three of them sat there for a few minutes making light conversation, then Sebastian got up decisively. 'I must go,' he said, then turned to look at Fleur. 'I'm going into Truro tomorrow morning—would you like to come? And you too, Pat,' he added as an afterthought. 'I know how you women like shopping.'

'It's kind of you to offer, Sebastian,' Pat said firmly, 'but I've lots of things to do and, besides, I want to be with Mum as much as possible. But Fleur will enjoy Truro—there's lots to see, apart from the shops.' She threw a shrewd glance at the two of them as she spoke. Sebastian had always been a bit of a dark horse where women were concerned, but she could definitely feel something in the air every time she caught him looking at Fleur. So *she* wasn't going to play gooseberry, thank you very much. Her expression softened as she looked at Sebastian. He was a good man, and a fantastic employer—as his parents had been—never overdemanding and always appreciative. And, although he had a bit of a short fuse at times, it was usually justified; he had a very keen sense of right and wrong. She knew Frank worshipped him, would do anything for him, and now Frank's son, Martin, always a bit of a tear-away, had come to work on the estate as well. And Sebastian had seen the youngster's potential as a carpenter and was paying for him to go part-time to college to learn the trade properly. But Fleur...this young woman...she could be just the one for Sebastian, Pat thought. She was different from other hopefuls who'd turned up occasionally at Pengarroth Hall... She seemed to sort of fit in with the atmosphere of the place, and to really enjoy being here and wandering about by herself. And she wasn't always looking at herself in the mirror, either.

'Oh, fine,' Sebastian said casually. 'How about you, Fleur? I promise there's enough to keep you interested while I'm seeing the accountant.'

She looked up at him. 'Are you sure it won't be rather inconvenient, thinking about me when you've got other more important things on your mind?' she asked.

He was just about to reply when Fleur's mobile rang, and she paused to answer it. It was Mia.

'Hi, Mia! Yes...fine, absolutely fine! Having a great time...and feeling great, too.' She smiled as she listened to her friend's exuberant tones. 'Oh, poor you, having to work so hard...but it'll be the same for me in just over a week...unless I'm called back earlier,' she added quickly, giving herself the option of cutting her stay short—and of letting Sebastian hear it. There was another pause, then, 'Yes, he's standing right here by my side. Do you want a word?'

She passed the phone up to Sebastian and listened as he and Mia exchanged the usual pleasantries. Then, 'Yes, you know that I always do as you tell me, and I'm taking Fleur into Truro tomorrow so that she can have a look around while I'm with the accountant and the solicitor. What? Oh, yes, we might do that as well... OK, OK, I'll pass you back. Be good.'

Fleur raised her eyebrows. *She* hadn't said she'd go with him—he was assuming that she would. But then, why not? she thought. She knew Truro wasn't that far away, and they'd only be gone for the morning...there'd still be plenty of day left for Sebastian after that, without having to think about her.

She watched his retreating back, then took their mugs over to the sink.

'Now, you leave those things to me, dear,' Pat said, thinking how pretty Fleur looked in her huge cream chunky sweater, her golden hair loose around her face. 'And, by the way, Mum says why don't you come up to the cottage for afternoon tea one day? Then you can bring back the novels she promised to lend you.'

'That would be great, Pat—thanks,' Fleur said. Pat's mother had been at the house for almost the whole of the three festive days, helping out, and she and Fleur had chatted, among other things, about their favourite authors. And when Fleur had said she was into romantic novels at the moment and had finished the one she'd brought with her, the older woman had offered to lend some of hers.

'Well, then, come up with me the day after tomorrow,' Pat said now, 'if you're going with Sebastian to Truro tomorrow.'

'I didn't say I was,' Fleur corrected. 'He did.' She smiled. 'But yes, I will go because I've never been to the city before—it is a city, isn't it, with a lovely cathedral? I mustn't pass up the opportunity to visit it.'

'You don't know Cornwall?' Pat asked curiously as she

started slicing thick pieces of gammon from a delicious-looking joint for their lunch.

'No, not really,' Fleur said. 'My father preferred Scotland and the Lakes, so we always went there when I was young. And in more recent years when I've been on holiday, it's to foreign countries with friends.' She paused. 'I must be the only person in the whole world who doesn't particularly look forward to going away. I'm much happier at home. But I have to, because that's what everyone does.' She watched Pat's deft handling of the carving knife, the pink ham glistening with succulence, making her mouth water even though it was a couple of hours before she'd be eating any. 'And thank your mother so much for the offer. She's an interesting lady, and I'd love to come to tea.'

Pat smiled, pleased. 'And I know she'll love it too,' she said. 'She doesn't see that many people any more and I think she's a bit lonely sometimes. See, even when Mia or Sebastian are away, I'm here most days, checking up, cleaning up, doing the odd bit of decorating where I see it's needed. And the kitchen garden round at the back is my domain too. Not that I do much to it this time of year,' she added.

Fleur stood up. 'I think I'll take Benson now. The weather seems reasonably fine, so maybe it's the best time of day to go.'

'You do that,' Pat said, giving the dog a gentle nudge with her toe. 'Get up, you lazy hound,' she said affectionately.

'What happens to him when you're not around?' Fleur wanted to know.

'Oh, he stays with Mum or me. Or Frank has him. He's well looked after. Up until a couple of years ago, Sebastian would take him back to London with him, but that proved impractical, and the dog pined a bit for home and hearth, I think.'

'Oh, well, then, Benson and I are of like mind.' Fleur smiled.

Pat finished what she was doing, then wrapped the remainder of the joint in cling film and put it in the fridge. 'Now, I'll prepare the lunch for one o'clock,' she said. 'Sebastian said he might be a bit later than that, but it'll all keep. And I'll take some of this on up and have mine with Mum.'

Fleur looked over at the bustling housekeeper as she spoke, hoping that Sebastian and Mia knew how lucky they were to have such devoted people to look after them and their property, whether they were here or not. Such staff would be hard to find in London. Everything here seemed so efficient, yet so easy-going.

Fleur took her warm jacket from the hook on the back door where she'd noticed that Sebastian always kept his, then called to Benson to follow her. And, surprisingly, the dog immediately got up and padded after her.

'See you later, Pat,' she called as they went outside. They set off, soon leaving the house behind them as they began treading up the soggy paths, the dog happy to lead the way, stopping and sniffing every few yards.

Thinking about it, Fleur still didn't know whether to say she'd been called back to the hospital or not… It was rather difficult now that she was going to Truro tomorrow, and to tea with Pat and her mother the day after. Which meant that there were only going to be five days left, in any case. She shrugged to herself. She'd see how things panned out. If she got the slightest suspicion that she was being a burden to Sebastian, or—perish the thought—that he was bored with her unasked-for company, she'd be gone within the hour. Until then no reason not to go with the flow, she told herself.

After half an hour or so of gentle strolling, she called out to the dog, who was investigating a scrubby bush. 'Have you had enough, Benson?' she called. 'Shall we turn back now? Good boy. Come on.'

The animal emerged reluctantly from whatever had held his interest, but continued on without even looking around at Fleur, who followed on behind him. Well, he was obviously enjoying himself, she thought.

And then, as usual and without much warning, a fine rain began again. She called out, more decisively this time, 'Come back, Benson…come *on*. We must go home now.' But, staying where he was, the dog merely turned and looked back soulfully at her.

Fleur sighed briefly. Pat had told her to take the lead, just in case, and now she went forward to attach it to the dog's collar. And, as if making a decision of his own, Benson sat down on the wet ground and refused to budge.

Fleur frowned, giving the lead a little pull. 'Come on, there's a good boy. We've had a lovely walk and it's time to go back. Come on, up you get.'

But the dog had other ideas, and after a few pointless moments of trying to persuade him, Fleur began to feel slightly worried. What if Benson refused to come home at all? He was much too heavy for her to pick up and carry. And if she went back alone, what would Sebastian's reaction be? She realized that the dog probably could make his own way home without any help from her, but that wasn't the point, and she couldn't take it for granted.

She crouched down by the dog. 'Well, have a little rest and then come with me, Benson, *please*,' she begged. She suddenly remembered that she had some mints in her pocket—maybe she could entice him with one of those. Getting up, she moved a few feet away and crackled the sweet paper between her fingers.

'Come and see, Benson. See what I've got,' she said cajolingly but, apart from a slight twitch of his nose, the dog expressed not the slightest interest.

'OK, then, we'll play it your way,' Fleur said. 'I'm going back now. See you later. Goodbye, Benson!' She turned away and started walking back in the direction they'd come, in the hope that the dog would follow her. But, as she turned to glance back, she could see that he hadn't moved an inch. He was not coming, and that was that.

Now Fleur was really exasperated. What now? she asked herself. She could not go home minus the dog; that would make her look silly. Glancing at her watch, she was horrified to see that it was almost one-thirty—they'd been gone far longer than she'd thought, or than she'd intended. But both she and her canine companion had been enjoying their walk so much that the time had slipped by. She shrugged. There was nothing else for it, she'd have to just wait and sit it out until Benson made up his mind to come home.

Feeling completely inadequate, she leaned against a tree for a few moments, then sat down on a piece of log a foot or two away from the dog. With her chin in her hands, she stared pensively at him and, hardly blinking, Benson stared back.

By now, the rain had become a steady downpour and both she and Benson were looking distinctly the worse for wear. Fleur had scarcely noticed that her hood had slipped off, or that her hair was hanging in wet ringlets around her face. 'No one warned me that you were a difficult creature, Benson,' she said sorrowfully. 'What on earth am I to do with you?'

'And what on earth am I to do with *you*?' Sebastian's voice intervened and, with an unmistakable sense of relief, Fleur saw him striding towards them. He stopped and looked down at her. 'What's going on?' he said. 'Pat's gone on home, but she did tell you she'd arranged lunch for one o'clock—didn't she?'

Fleur didn't bother to get to her feet, but nodded towards Benson, who was viewing them both pensively. 'Ask him,' she said. 'He just refused to get up. I couldn't leave him here, could I?' She sighed. 'I must be rubbish at handling dogs.'

Sebastian cocked one slightly amused eyebrow, then clicked his fingers. 'Come, Benson,' he said masterfully, and at once the dog got to his feet and padded over to lick his hand.

Fleur could hardly believe it! The naughty animal, she thought. He'd seemed rooted to that spot, yet two words from Sebastian and he'd obeyed at once. 'Obviously it's his master's voice that he responds to,' she said sniffily, getting up and falling into step with Sebastian as they began to make their way home.

'No, I think the fact was he was enjoying your company so much, he didn't want the walk to end,' Sebastian said generously, glancing down at her. She was soaking wet, her hair looking as if she had just come out of the shower, and he smiled faintly to himself. Not many of the women he'd known had shown such stalwart tendencies, usually running for cover at the first brush with the elements. But Fleur seemed to almost revel in being wet and untidy.

It took another half an hour to get back, with Benson now trotting quite happily ahead. 'I don't believe that dog,' Fleur said. 'Look at him. What did I do wrong?'

'Nothing,' Sebastian replied. 'I expect he just felt like a

lie down, that's all—you had gone quite a way—much further than I usually take him nowadays.'

Fleur looked up quickly. 'Oh, dear…I hope we didn't overdo it…I mean, I don't want to be the cause of any trouble…'

'Shut up,' Sebastian said cheerfully. 'The dog's fine. The only one suffering any discomfort is me, because you've kept me waiting for my lunch.'

'Well, why didn't you go on and have it without me?' Fleur began.

'What, knowing that my dog and my…er…*charge*… were missing, believed lost?'

Fleur decided to ignore the word he'd used because she knew he was teasing her.

Back at the house, she had a quick wash, then took her place opposite Sebastian at the kitchen table. He had placed the ham and pickles and the piping hot, gloriously brown jacket potatoes in front of them, and soon they were both tucking into it all, while Benson lay flat out on the floor, snoring.

Without asking her whether she wanted any, Sebastian filled Fleur's glass with water from the jug, before taking some for himself. She was glad that there was no wine on offer because, as she'd already told him, she seldom drank alcohol during the day. That must have made her sound terribly goody-goody, she thought, because most of her friends had no problem with having a glass or two at lunch time. But she didn't care what Sebastian Conway thought of her, anyway—about anything at all—she'd always made a point of never altering her principles to suit others, and she wasn't about to start now.

Finishing his lunch, he asked mildly, 'What are you

going to do with yourself this afternoon?' He realized that it wasn't a polite enquiry, but he was curious and admitted that he would much rather spend the rest of the day with Fleur than helping Frank. But suddenly the phone on the wall rang and he stood up to take the call. It was Pat and, after listening for a few moments and glancing across at Fleur, he said, 'No, you must stay with her, Pat… That's no problem. For heaven's sake, we can cope alone, sort ourselves out.' There was a pause. 'Sorry? Oh, yes…of course. I found them…up Middle Hill. Yes, right up there. Soaking wet, with Benson having gone on strike. He didn't want to come home, apparently. But they're both here, safe and well, and we've just enjoyed the lunch—thanks, Pat.' Another pause. 'Absolutely not—you stay with Beryl. We'll be fine.' He listened again, then, 'OK, got it. And it's best you don't come back tonight at all—your mother needs you more than we do just now. See what the doctor says, and we'll see you tomorrow some time, when the panic's over. OK? Cheers, Pat.'

He replaced the receiver. 'Pat's mother has just had another of her angina attacks, so I've told her that we can look after ourselves for twenty-four hours.'

'Of course we can,' Fleur said at once.

'And apparently we're having steak for our supper—they're in the 'fridge, along with mushrooms and tomatoes and stuff…' He eyed her hopefully. 'Can you cook? I'm not the greatest,' he added.

'Well, then, you'd better leave it all to me,' Fleur said, realizing how quickly she and her host had become so…so comfortable with each other, with no pressure, no emotional vibes cutting into the warmly pleasant atmosphere they seemed to be enjoying. Well, what else did she expect?

He was Mia's brother. She had always loved her friend…and she was beginning to love him, as well…in a purely brotherly way, naturally, she assured herself. 'Not that I shall hope to come up to Pat's standards,' she went on, 'but beggars can't be choosers. It's me or nothing.'

He treated her to one of his rather enigmatic smiles. 'You'll do nicely,' he murmured.

She took their empty plates over to the sink, thinking that he needn't concern himself. She'd always enjoyed cooking, and she knew she could produce a meal to satisfy anyone. And she'd bet anything that he'd like his steak cooked rare.

He turned to go. 'Right, I'll be back up the top with Frank for the rest of the day.' He paused. 'You don't envisage wearing my dog's paws out again, do you?'

'No. I shall be having a long, hot bath and washing my hair.' She made a slight grimace, knowing that she must be looking totally scruffy after the morning's drenching. 'After which, I might watch a DVD, and then think about our supper.'

He stopped to look down at her, suddenly feeling a wave of pleasure sweep through him. It would be rather good to think of coming home to Fleur after a heavy day outside, he thought, for them to share a meal and just sit and relax and chat. And to have her here, all to himself, at Pengarroth Hall. As he dwelt on that for a second or two, and despite his avowed intention to watch it where women were concerned, a ripple of anticipation coursed through his veins and stopped him in his tracks. It had been a long time since he'd experienced these sensual instincts. The need to be with a woman, close enough to touch, and it had taken this rather unusual friend of Mia's to make him realize how much he'd missed it!

CHAPTER FIVE

'WELL, *that* was a surprise,' Sebastian said as he and Fleur were relaxing in the sitting room after supper. 'Eleven out of ten for the way you did my steak, Fleur—thanks.'

He glanced across at her as he spoke. Curled up as she was on the sofa, with her knees drawn up comfortably and her eyes closed, she looked ridiculously at ease.

'I'll take that as a compliment, rather than an insult, if you mean that you were surprised I didn't ruin that wonderful meat,' Fleur said drowsily.

When he'd returned late in the afternoon, he'd lit the fire and now the logs were crackling and hissing in the flames. With the lamps turned down low, the room was swathed in a gentle, soothing light, adding to the contented atmosphere which both of them were very much aware of. Sitting opposite her in one of the huge armchairs, he was wearing chinos and a light open-neck sports shirt, his bare feet thrust into loafers, his long legs stretched out in front of him.

He was quietly amazed at how totally comfortable he felt in Fleur's company—as if he'd known her for ages. She was certainly the only woman he'd ever met who didn't send out the usual signals that he was accustomed to receiving— the telling eye contact or suggestive comment, or any kind of simple gesture that told him she might fancy him. He thought she seemed to quite *like* him, but nothing more than that—and that pleased him. Because it made it easier for him to keep her emotionally at arm's length. Neither of them—certainly not him—were interested in having a meaningful relationship with anyone, so that obviously explained why there was no tension, he thought. He smiled faintly to himself. The only slight problem was that she was so attractive… It would have helped if he could have looked at her dispassionately, but there was no hope of that. Still, soon they'd be going their separate ways and he doubted that he'd ever see her again. All of their lives, his and Mia's and their respective friends, were so busy these days, it was difficult for any of them to get together.

He'd brought in the half-empty bottle of wine they'd shared the evening before, and now he leaned forward to refill their glasses, glancing across at her. He didn't want her to go to sleep—which she seemed in imminent danger of doing—he wanted her to talk to him, wanted to hear some more of her opinions.

'I take it you've no objection to helping me out with the remains of this?' he enquired.

Still not moving, she opened her eyes lazily. 'All right, but please make it a small one,' she murmured. 'I don't have a very strong head for alcohol, but it was delicious.'

She watched his strong, completely steady, tanned hand pour the ruby liquid. He placed the bottle down on the small, low table in front of them with a gentle thud. 'Good. That's a dead one,' he said. 'But there's plenty more we can open if you feel like living dangerously.'

She smiled back at him. 'No, thanks. But I won't say no to a coffee. I'll go out and make some in a minute.'

He drank some wine, then leaned back, twirling the glass in his fingers. 'No, you stay there. You look so comfortable, it would be a crime to disturb you. I'll make the coffee, since you did everything else.'

There was silence for a few moments, then, 'You said your parents were holidaying in Boston,' he said. 'Have you heard from them?'

'Oh, yes, they rang me on New Year's Day with the usual good wishes... Well, my father hoped I'd have another successful, fulfilling and productive year ahead, but my mother's greetings centred more on fun and happiness.' She smiled faintly. 'She's desperate for me to provide her with a grandchild, drops hints all the time—when my father's not around—but it's never likely to happen, I'm afraid. I've never actually said that to her, of course, because it sounds rather cruel, but I fear she hopes in vain.'

Sebastian looked at her seriously for a moment. 'You don't like kids?' he said.

'Of course I like children,' Fleur replied at once. 'What I don't relish is having to hand my life over to their father, to become anonymous.' She shook her head quickly. Her mother was a beautiful, gifted woman and had become like a silent, wistful bird in a cage—or so it seemed to Fleur. There was no way she was going to suffer the same fate, to be controlled by a man. Her father had done enough already to utterly convince her of that.

Sebastian didn't need any further explanation. Fleur's deep-rooted resentment about certain influences in her life had tarnished the natural inclination most women had for matrimonial commitment and child-bearing. He stared at her thoughtfully. What a waste, he mused. She was clearly an intelligent woman, who'd produce beautiful children.

After a few moments he left the room, returning with the coffee things on a tray, which he set down on the table.

'Sugar and cream for madam,' he said briefly, passing them to her, and pouring himself a black coffee. Fleur leaned forward, not surprised that he'd obviously noted what she liked, without having to ask. He was that kind of man.

Stirring her drink slowly, she said, 'Soon this will all be a distant memory.' She smiled up at him briefly. 'I've kept a diary so that I can refer back.'

'Well, you can always come and visit again,' he said casually. 'Whether Mia's here or not. It's good for the house to be used, and Pat's always around... You'd be more than welcome, any time.' That was a first, he thought—telling one of his sister's friends to make herself at home! He paused. 'You'd love it when all the spring flowers are in bloom.... Our bluebell woods are something else—in fact, we have a bluebell event every year, the first weekend in May. Everyone around comes to admire our carpets of blue, and we lay on a bit of a tea in the garden and the kids are invited to pick primroses to take home.'

Fleur's eyes sparkled as she listened to the picture he had just painted. 'How fantastic!' she exclaimed. 'I *love* bluebells—not to pick, of course, because they don't last once they leave the ground, but they're always such a magical sight.' She paused. 'I'd *love* to see it—perhaps one day, if Mia's coming down, we could drive here together.'

'It doesn't matter whether Mia's coming or not,' he repeated. 'Though she usually does put in an appearance. I always make a point of being here because it's the only occasion when anyone and everyone is welcome to explore the estate...and it's good for community spirit, that sort of thing. I'm often glad of local help to give Frank a hand from time to time, so it's in my interests to be convivial now and then.'

They fell silent for a few moments, then Fleur said suddenly, 'On Christmas Eve, when the others were all here, everyone started telling ghost stories, and Mia said that...'

'Oh, she told you about our supernatural presence, did she?' he asked good-humouredly. 'Well, it's kept many a guest entertained after dinner.'

'But—there isn't *really* a ghost, is there?' Fleur said, keeping her voice totally expressionless, even though her pulse had quickened at the thought. 'I thought she was pulling our legs.'

'None of *us* have seen him, certainly,' Sebastian replied easily. 'But there are accounts of others having had the experience.' He drank from his mug, then looked over at her. 'Why, that sort of thing doesn't bother you, does it? You don't believe such nonsense?'

'Of course not,' Fleur said loftily. 'I'm a scientist. I only believe what I can see or prove. And, to my knowledge, no one has yet proved the existence of such beings, have they? I mean, they may *believe* they've seen certain things, but that's not the same thing as actually seeing or touching— with others there to corroborate, is it? It's just all in the mind. Still,' she added, 'tell me more. Because Mia had hardly started telling us when Mandy nearly had hysterics at the thought, so she had to stop.'

Sebastian leaned back, his hands behind his head. 'Well, our ghost is apparently a well-dressed middle-aged man who wears a top hat. He's been seen walking along the upstairs landing, hangs around a bit as if he's waiting for someone to join him, then walks straight out through the wall at the end.'

Fleur gave a slightly sardonic smile. 'How bizarre.' She paused. 'Who's supposed to have seen him, anyway?'

'One of our forebears made a note of it a hundred years ago—it's quoted briefly in the official documents,' Sebastian replied. 'Since then two others have declared they've witnessed it. One was a young lad, the tea boy, who was boiling a kettle upstairs to make some drinks for the decorators my parents had employed to do some work. Someone must have said something to him about our ghost and the lad swore he saw it do the disappearing trick through the wall. Anyway, he dropped the kettle and fled out of the house, refusing to come back in.' Sebastian chortled at the thought. 'But then there's also…'

'Who else has seen it?' Fleur interrupted eagerly.

'Beryl, Pat's mother, swears she's seen it too, twice—when she's been upstairs cleaning.'

Fleur caught her breath. '*Beryl's* seen it?' she said. 'Really?' This was different. The woman was a practical no-nonsense character and, in Fleur's opinion, not likely to make up things about seeing visions.

'Yep. So she insists,' Sebastian said cheerfully. 'But she has no problem with it at all. Says that as long as the chap doesn't give her any aggro or get under her feet, she's quite happy to see him now and again.' He chuckled. 'Mind you, I have to say that Beryl's private remedy for any ailment she might be suffering from is a rather good elderberry wine she makes. And I'm pretty certain that she enjoys a daily dose—which might explain things—not that I've ever seen her the worse for wear.'

'Well, so Mia *wasn't* having us on, then,' Fleur said slowly. She sat back and feigned a yawn, feeling undeniably uncomfortable. What she had just said about not believing in the supernatural wasn't entirely true because, in spite of her training, she knew there were still certain things which seemed to have no rational explanation. Phenomena whose secrets were yet to be revealed... Of course, it would all become clear one day, she was sure of that. There were so many more curtains to push back in order to find the truth behind the myriad unanswered questions.

'My mother would find your ghost absolutely fascinating,' she said, looking across at Sebastian. She paused. 'She is what you would call a...spiritual person, with a very open mind. Though of course my father scoffs at anything which isn't firmly rooted in proven fact.'

'And you agree with him, obviously,' Sebastian said.

After a second's thought, she replied, 'Yes. Of course.'

'What about horoscopes—you don't read them either?' he persisted. 'I know that Mia does—it's the first page she turns to when I see her with a magazine. And she's totally unashamed to admit it. She'll say things like, "Oh, good, someone special is going to enter my life this week," or "Hurrah—I'm coming into unexpected money!"'

Fleur smiled across at him. 'And what about you— where do you stand on all this?' she enquired.

'I never read women's mags, that's for sure,' he replied, 'and I've never read my horoscope either, though Mia has often insisted on looking up my sign and telling me what's in store for me in the imminent future.'

Neither of them spoke for a few moments, then Fleur got up, stretching her arms above her head. 'I really must go to bed now,' she said. ' I think I had too much supper, and too much wine...' She bent to pick up the tray. 'I'll just clear this up first.' She glanced across at him. 'When do you want me to be ready in the morning? I mean…you said you've appointments in Truro…'

He stifled a yawn too then, and got slowly to his feet. 'We should leave at nine.' He smiled. 'Do you want an early morning call?'

'That won't be necessary,' Fleur replied. 'I always wake up with the birds.' Though she had to admit that almost since her first day here she'd slept like a log, not rousing until much later than usual. The stress she'd been experiencing for the last few months, which had been the cause of disturbed nights and early waking, seemed to have vanished.

'I'll say goodnight, then, Sebastian,' she said, turning to go.

'Goodnight, Fleur—sleep well,' he added.

Up in her room, Fleur undressed quickly and, after a quick wash and cleaning her teeth, she burrowed beneath her duvet. Glancing over to the other single bed, she wished that Mia was still there. It had been very comfortable, the two of them together, nattering away about everything—old times, new plans—until one or other had been the first to fall asleep. Now, the room seemed very still with only her own breathing to keep her company. She'd heard Sebastian come upstairs and pass her room, had listened to his firm tread receding for several moments. She didn't know which bedroom he occupied, only that it seemed to be away at the far end of the wide landing.

Sighing briefly, she snuggled down.

And that night Fleur dreamed, her subconscious mind teeming with thoughts, events, voices, memories and feelings… For several hours, she tossed and turned restlessly. In her dreams, she and her mother were having one of their discussions about other-worldly things, about

Helen's inexplicable forebodings, which often turned out to have some verity, about the second sense which she seemed to possess, about the angels that she implicitly believed were all around… And then, without any warning, and with a huge wave of anxiety sweeping over her, Fleur sat bolt upright, her forehead spangled with perspiration. Because she was no longer alone! She could see him—he *did* exist! The ghost of Pengarroth Hall, his top hat firmly on his head, was right there in her room, and he was walking slowly towards her! Pulling the duvet right up around her shoulders, she opened her mouth to say something, to cry out, to tell it to go away and leave her alone! But no words would come! Her tongue had stuck fast to her dry mouth, rendering her impotent and helpless… She was his prisoner and she was trapped with no means of escape. With her shaking knees drawn up to her chin, her eyes huge with fright, she watched him come nearer and nearer all the time, and suddenly…suddenly…amazingly…she recognized him… It was her father—her *father* was here! But how…why? She could make out the familiar features, the determined expression, the permanently puckered brow, and at last Fleur did find her voice and she screamed, *'No! Go away! You shouldn't be here! Leave me alone—leave me alone!'* But the figure kept on walking and Fleur kept on screaming a high-pitched, frantic scream until, cowering now, she could almost feel him, he was so close… Suddenly the door burst open and Sebastian stood there, a look of shocked disbelief on his face.

'Fleur… *Fleur!* What the hell is it?' He strode right over to the bed and, without a second's hesitation, she sprang up into a kneeling position and clutched him feverishly around his neck, almost bowling him over in her desperation to feel him near her. And with that human contact, feeling the comforting warmth of his bare chest against her flimsily clad form, she burst into tears. Helpless, hopeless tears. Tears partly of shock, partly of relief—and partly of release. She could not remember the last time she'd cried—it must have been years and years ago, and she sobbed unashamedly.

Sebastian let her cry, saying not another word, but now sitting down on the bed with her, his arms wrapped around her, his chin resting on the top of her head.

'I saw him...I did see him,' she gasped tremulously between sobs, and he held her even closer to him.

'Hush, Fleur...it's OK...you're OK. I'm here...' he murmured.

Afterwards, she couldn't recall how long they'd stayed like that, but eventually her tears began to lessen and she raised her eyes to look up at him. And then, as if it were the obvious, natural sequence of events, his mouth came down upon her lips—lips that were parted with the effort of trying to breathe normally after her anguished weeping. And the moist warmth of that brief union sent thrilling waves coursing down her spine... She didn't pull away, she didn't *want* to pull away because, in a kind of wonder, she found herself glowing in this intimate contact, Sebastian's overt masculinity making her feel desired, wanted, protected...but not overpowered. Not threatened in any way. And, as her terror finally died, she stayed quite still in his arms, not wanting him to leave her. Amazingly, she felt no embarrassment that they had kissed like that, no shyness that she had felt his body harden against her, had felt the muscles of his broad shoulders tense against her fingers as she'd clutched him to her.

Eventually, reluctantly, he drew away and said softly,

'Fleur, you did not see anything… You've just had a horrible dream, that's all, and I'm really sorry that I told you about the wretched ghost… It was a silly thing to do, just before going to bed.' He gazed down at her for a long moment… Her brief nightwear exposed her slight shoulders and the cleft of her smooth breasts, her hair tangled and damp. Gently, he pulled a lock of it away from her forehead, smoothing his fingers across her cheek for a second. Then, reaching across, he took a tissue from a box on the bedside table and carefully wiped away her tears.

Fully awake—and aware—now, Fleur suddenly became very conscious that he was clad only in dark boxer shorts, conscious of the black hair on his bare chest, of his broad, muscular thighs, and she shivered briefly. Was this part of the dream, would she wake up in a minute and find him gone? But she knew it was no fantasy… His throbbing body, melding with hers, was no figment of her imagination.

After a moment of trying to control his own heightened awareness, he murmured, 'Do you want me to stay?' He paused, feeling a surging, burgeoning hope that she would say yes.

But, after a second's hesitation, she replied, 'No…no, there's no need, thank you…I'm fine now, really. And I'm so sorry.' She swallowed, taking the damp tissue from him and dabbing at her eyes. 'Of course you're right, Sebastian. I was dreaming. How could it possibly have been anything else? But I'm sorry I disturbed you, sorry that you had to come and…and sort me out…'

He smiled briefly, releasing her gently, and got up straight away and went over to the door, glancing back at the crestfallen woman half-kneeling, half-crouching on the bed. 'Can I make you a warm drink, Fleur? Something to help you get back to sleep?' he said quietly.

She returned his smile, beginning to feel calm and more in possession of her self-control. 'No, thanks. I'll have a glass of water and take one of my tablets,' she said. 'I'll…I'll sleep now, Sebastian. And I really do apologize for being such an idiot.'

He nodded at that, going out and closing the door softly behind him.

On his way back to his own room, he was aware that his nerves had quickened dangerously, making him feel frustrated and edgy, and he cursed under his breath. It would have only taken one word from her to make him slide into that bed beside her and take and hold her in his arms, and make tender, unhurried love to her until dawn broke. How had she managed that? Would he really have succumbed that easily? There may not have been any ghost about, but she'd certainly cast a spell on him!

He went into his own room and shut the door, leaning against it for a second. Thank heavens she'd turned down his offer to spend the rest of the night with her. He must have been out of his mind to suggest it. He went across to the window and stared out moodily into the darkness for a moment. He'd thought he was impervious to the lure of beautiful, vulnerable women—but obviously not. Well, it had been a timely warning to keep his distance! And especially with this one, and for whom his restless body still ached. Would he *never* learn?

CHAPTER SIX

FLEUR stood for several moments, staring at the small bottle of tablets in her hand. She knew she wasn't going to take any—because she didn't want her mind to become even slightly numbed, or hazy, about what had just happened. She wanted the memory, the sensation of Sebastian's mouth hard on hers to stay with her for as long as possible. She wanted to feel his strong arms around her, she wanted the manly fragrance of him to linger in her nostrils.

She glanced at herself in the bathroom mirror—what a sight she looked. Her face was pale and tear-stained, her hair a tangled mess of damp waves, yet that hadn't seemed to matter to Sebastian. She knew that he had wanted her just now—even looking like this—he had wanted her badly, and it had taken all her common sense and control to deny him. And to deny herself, she admitted. Because for those few moments her need had been as acute as his. How had she managed to send him away?

She frowned slightly… What a bizarre thing to have happened, she thought…that their 'ghost' should have suddenly taken on her father's face… What on earth was that all about? Then she shrugged. That was the thing with dreams and nightmares. They *were* bizarre, and had no rhyme or reason.

She filled a glass with water and drank freely. She knew very well how she had managed to resist Sebastian. Even though he had been so kind and thoughtful…and gentle… she knew him to be yet another powerful man, an important man whose self-worth was never in doubt, used to giving orders and to being in command. To having things his way. The very sort she didn't want to become involved with, to have any meaningful relationship with. And, anyway, something he'd once said had made it clear that he wasn't the committing sort either. So that was all right then, she thought. His philosophy would undoubtedly be to enjoy any fleeting moment of passion and pass on unhindered.

Slowly, she climbed back into bed. Tomorrow was another day, and tonight's little episode must be forgotten, ignored, as quickly as possible. She was sorry that she'd accepted his offer of a trip to Truro, but when he was otherwise engaged she'd invent the phone call asking her to return to London. It was safer to get back, to get away from Pengarroth Hall.

She did, finally, drift off to sleep and this time her dreams were pure luxury. Sebastian was there all the time beside her, cradling her in his arms, caressing her in a way that no one had ever done before. It was comforting, it was calm…it was exquisite.

When she woke up, she felt refreshed and resolute. That ridiculous nightmare had resulted in her behaving in an unbelievable way. She'd allowed Sebastian—her host, after all, and Mia's brother—to kiss her passionately, in very intimate circumstances. What they'd been wearing had left nothing to the imagination!

She showered and put on jeans and the silver-grey sloppy sweater which her mother had given her for Christmas. Then she brushed her hair up into a knot on top, touched up her face lightly with blusher and a hint of eye-shadow, and went downstairs.

She could hear Sebastian already in the kitchen and as she opened the door she felt her heart lurch inexplicably. Upstairs, she'd felt so confident of herself, of her feelings, of her determination, so sure that she could appear as if nothing special had gone on last night, and now her legs felt as if they belonged to someone else.

He was at the stove with his back to her as she entered, and he immediately turned to face her, fleeting admiration in his eyes as he took in her appearance. But then his ex-pression changed almost immediately and, clearing his throat, he turned back to making the coffee. 'Morning,' he said briefly. 'Did you manage to sleep OK—eventually?'

'Yes, thank you, I had a good night in the end.' She went over to the fridge. 'Would you like me to cook you something—eggs poached, boiled or fried?' she asked casually, as if she was asking the question of just anyone rather than the man who could have seduced her last night if he'd wanted to.

He put the lid firmly on the percolator, then took it across to the table, where he had already laid two mugs and plates. 'No, I seldom eat breakfast,' he said, pulling out a chair to sit down, 'but you carry on if you want to.'

'Just some toast will be fine for me,' she said. She paused. 'Shall I make some for you as well?'

'Go on, then. I'll keep you company,' he replied.

Making enough for both of them, she brought it over to the table, together with some butter and a jar of home-made honey, then sat down opposite him. Raising her eyes briefly, she said matter-of-factly, 'I really must apologize for last night, Sebastian. I don't know what came over me.' She paused to butter the toast carefully. 'I'm very sorry that you were disturbed.'

He was about to say, *I wasn't sorry...not a bit*. How could any red-blooded male feel regret at being allowed to kiss a delectable woman in the middle of the night? Then he thought better of it. It was different today—totally, utterly different. She was cool, composed, almost indifferent towards him. He wondered whether she remembered that he'd held her so closely, that she'd given him her lips so willingly. Perhaps that, too, by now had become part of her dreaming, he thought.

'There's absolutely no need to apologize,' he said smoothly. 'If I'd waited for just a few more moments, you'd have recovered by yourself, and there would have been no need for me to...intrude...on your privacy. But...' he paused '...when I heard you calling out, I did feel that I should at least enquire. The comfort of our guests is always paramount at Pengarroth Hall.'

His remarks were neatly put, Fleur had to give him that. He *might* have said, *When I heard you screaming your head off, I thought you were being murdered*. Or something like it.

'The strange thing is, I don't think I usually have nightmares,' she said, 'but, as I sleep alone, there's no one who could confirm that.' She shook her head briefly. 'But last night that ghost seemed so very real... How the mind can play stupid tricks sometimes.' She pretended to giggle, to be amused, but there had been nothing amusing about the effect it had had on her. She had been utterly terrified. Still, there was no need to prolong the experience by going on and on about it. She decided to change the subject. 'So, you have meetings today,' she said, biting into her slice of toast. 'Do you expect to have lengthy discussions?'

'Oh, I shouldn't be too long,' he said, 'but it's always hard to tell. I fully expect to be able to pick you up in time for some lunch.' He picked up his mug. 'We've got some literature hanging about somewhere, about Truro—I know there's plenty to keep you interested there while I'm gone.' He glanced over to her as he drank his coffee. He couldn't believe that their physical encounter last night was being totally disregarded today. As if it had never happened. When anything so stirringly emotional as that had taken place, it was usual for those involved to acknowledge that it had happened—by a word or a gesture. But…that was good, wasn't it? he asked himself. It fitted in with his plans exactly as he wanted it to. He wanted to forget the feel of Fleur's body enveloped in his. Wanted to forget the tide of feeling which had hit him with the force of a tsunami as he'd claimed her sweet, moist lips. And she was clearly of the same mind because the emotional distance between them now was vast—and obvious. It was clearly going to be the host/guest relationship from now on. So—that was good…wasn't it?

'Yes, I noticed the leaflets about Truro on the table in the hall,' she said, 'and, from what I could see, I don't expect to have time to fit it all in. Quite apart from visiting the cathedral and the museum—and all the shops, of course—I just like wandering around places I don't know, walking along the alleys and side streets, getting a feel of how a place ticks. I even like peeping in at people's windows,' she admitted. She smiled across at him quickly. 'So please don't give me a thought, or worry that I may be at a loose end. I assure you, I shan't be.'

'OK, that's fine,' he said casually. 'But I'll ring you on your mobile as soon as the meeting's over, and come and pick you up, wherever you happen to be.' He paused. 'There are plenty of coffee houses for you to refresh yourself, but we'll have some lunch at a rather special place later.' He threw her a glance. 'Mia instructed me on the phone that I must take you there, so I'd better do as she says.'

Fleur stirred some cream into her coffee thoughtfully for a moment. 'You don't have to do that, Sebastian—really you don't. Why waste any more time in Truro?' She hoped she wasn't sounding offhand or ungrateful, but it still rankled with her that Mia had more or less put him in a corner, to 'look after' her. She was quite all right on her own—as she'd tried to convince him before.

'Oh, we might as well have lunch before we head back,' he said casually. 'I'll be hungry, even if you aren't. And, by the way,' he added, 'Pat rang earlier—her mother's much better, apparently, so she'll be back to take up the reins again tonight.' He paused. 'I did tell her that we were managing OK on our own, but she's very possessive of her position here, and I didn't want to make her feel unnecessary, or unwanted…so I didn't try and persuade her to stay at their cottage for a bit longer. Anyway, that means you won't be on supper duty tonight.'

Fleur looked across at him as he spoke. Despite his overtly purposeful nature, and undoubtedly rather imperious streak at times, he was always thoughtful. Even if on their very first encounter he'd made her feel as small as a five penny piece. But she must forget that, she told herself. First impressions, though often valid, did not tell the whole story. As had been proved!

She suddenly remembered the dog. 'Where's Benson?' she asked.

'Oh, Frank's got him.' Sebastian poured himself another coffee. 'And then Pat'll be here later on.'

Soon they were ready to leave and, going outside, Fleur saw that Sebastian had brought his car around to the front door. It was the latest BMW model, a hazy, sensuous blue-grey, and she smiled up at him as he opened the passenger door for her. 'This is…rather… beautiful,' she said. 'A slightly more elevated specimen than my own car,' she added. She'd not seen her car since arriving—Sebastian had parked it for her in the garages, which were obviously around the back somewhere.

'Your car is a very sensible size,' he said, 'especially if you don't need to use the motorways too much. Perfect for London.'

For only the second time since she'd been here, the sun started to break warily through the grey skies and, as Sebastian drove smoothly along the drive, Fleur's spirits rose with every turn of the wheels. She loved a day out, to go somewhere different, and in spite of her misgivings about Sebastian—as well as her own deep-seated feelings—being with this outstandingly-good looking, elegant man certainly put the icing on the cake! She gave him a sidelong glance. He was dressed formally in a sharp suit, plain shirt and knotted tie—the perfect picture of British masculinity, she thought. And his rugged profile, hinting at just an element of harshness, seemed to confirm her view of him as possessing a many-layered personality. Then she amended her thoughts slightly. No, not harsh, she decided…just faintly mysterious, as though no human being would ever be able to reach the real man, to get to the very heart and soul of him. She turned to look steadily ahead.

It took less than an hour to get to Truro and, after they'd exchanged mobile numbers, Sebastian pulled into the car park of the offices he was visiting. 'As soon as I'm done,' he said, glancing across at her, 'I'll ring and come and find you.' He smiled slowly at her as she got out. 'Have fun,' he murmured.

For the next hour or so, Fleur strolled through the streets, lapping up the atmosphere of the ancient city. Even in early January, there were plenty of tourists about. She soon came upon the County District Offices, and the new Crown Courts, wondering idly whether Sebastian had ever had to flex his professional muscles there. But it was the cathedral that dominated the city centre as it gazed down authoritatively on the Georgian streets that meandered and weaved their way through the city.

Wandering on she came to the two covered markets which were thriving and busy as they set out to encourage early shoppers, but it was Lemon Quay's Creation Centre that Fleur knew would absorb her interest. It was a fascinating arcade, housing specialist shops which were calling out to be explored. This was a holiday experience she certainly hadn't known she'd be enjoying—spending time at the shops! With her head on one side thoughtfully, she assessed the well-dressed windows, wondering whether to buy anything. She seldom shopped much in London, not unless she really needed something, so just wandering about and not having to worry about what time it was added to her sense of freedom and well-being.

In the end, she bought a dainty silver bracelet to take

back to her mother, and some unusual embossed note-paper for herself, then decided that she would get some-thing for Pat and Beryl as well. But what? she wondered. She didn't know either woman well enough to know their tastes. She'd have to go on thinking, and hope for inspiration.

She stopped for a few minutes for coffee in one of the small restaurants before deciding to go into the cathedral. Although she knew it to be one of the newest in the country—work only starting on it in 1880—that did not detract from its powerful grandeur or sense of history, its towers and spires dominating everything around it.

Just before she decided to go in, her mobile rang. 'I'm finished here,' Sebastian said. 'Where are you?'

'About to go into the cathedral.'

'OK. I'll come in and find you.'

As soon as she set foot inside, Fleur was struck by how large and wide it was, its slender pillars and tiers of pointed arches automatically making her look upwards to the vaulted roof. There were other visitors looking around too, and presently Fleur trod quietly along the nave, musing at how many sacred buildings like this there must be around the world, places of sanctuary and worship. And, for a reason she couldn't explain, a huge lump formed in her throat. But it was the sudden magical music from the organ as it spilled out and filled every corner of the building with its awesome sound that took Fleur's breath right away. That majestic instrument of praise echoed and re-echoed around, so that every single stone and pillar might hear the timeless messages of hope, solace and inspiration.

She decided to sit down for a few moments, closing her

eyes and conscious that a solitary tear was drifting slowly down her cheek. Followed by one or two more.

And then…Sebastian moved in to sit quietly beside her and, without saying a word, he touched her arm gently. Quickly opening her eyes, she saw that he was offering her his handkerchief and she took it from him, touching her face with it briefly. He looked down at her quizzically.

'These places can get to you, can't they?' he said unexpectedly.

'Oh…they make you feel so small, so insignificant, so…pointless, somehow,' she replied with a small smile.

He was still looking at her, and his expression had softened as she spoke. 'I think it's high time I bought you some lunch. Come on. You've done enough soliloquizing.'

He took her arm and drew her to her feet. 'I've had a very successful morning,' he whispered cheerfully. 'All problems laid to rest.'

She smiled up at him quickly, glad to be brought back down to earth. 'Oh, that's great,' she said, automatically thinking that whatever the 'problems' were, they would undoubtedly have been solved to his advantage. It would take a very strong person—whoever he was—to get the better of Sebastian Conway.

'We're going to eat at a very special inn—one that my sister and I have visited several times,' he said, as they arrived outside, 'but we mustn't overdo it because Pat's cooking for us later, remember.'

And it *was* special, Fleur thought as they entered. It had a robust atmosphere but it was obviously a well-run and welcoming place. They found a convenient corner table by a window and, while Sebastian was ordering some drinks at the bar, Fleur gazed outside at the busy streets, the comings and goings of passers-by. She felt almost dizzy with contentment as she glanced over at Sebastian's lean, athletic figure, the handsome head held high, and suddenly he glanced back at *her* and their eyes met in a way that she would remember for a long time. Then he came back with a lemonade for her and a lager for himself, and handed her the menu.

'I recommend the crab sandwiches,' he said, 'which are very generous and served with an amazing salad…but if you want anything cooked, then the steak and beer pie is equally wonderful, though somewhat filling.'

Fleur smiled up at him. 'Crab sandwiches will suit me very well,' she said happily.

When the food came, it was absolutely delicious and after she'd finished it Fleur unashamedly ran a forefinger around her plate to mop up the last bit of the dressing. 'Yummy,' she said softly, looking up at him gratefully. 'Thank you.'

Yummy was a word he might have used to describe *her*, he thought. Why did she look so good in everything she wore, and why did those soft eyes with that occasional lazy blink affect him every time…? For crying out loud, this was a Monday morning in early January, he'd just sat through nearly three hours of an important business meeting, and yet all that was consuming his interest was the beautiful woman sitting opposite him. He pulled himself together. She was going home next week, and she'd be out of his life. Why waste his feelings on a ship that would pass in the night? Or waste his feelings on *any* woman? He'd already made his mind up about that—and he seldom, if ever, changed his mind about important issues. It was not in his nature.

After their meal they wandered back to the car and

Sebastian drove them home—much more slowly than he would have done if he had been alone. He'd enjoyed himself much, much more than he could have imagined. Enjoyed being with Fleur. And when he'd thrown out the invitation to take her with him to Truro, he'd only really done it to satisfy Mia.

'Oh, I forgot something! Can you…is there…?' Fleur interrupted his thoughts.

He turned and looked at her briefly. 'Why—what is it? What have you forgotten?'

She tutted to herself, irritated. 'I wanted to buy some little gift for Pat—and her mother,' she said. 'Going into the cathedral pushed everything else out of my mind. I meant to do it later. They've both been so kind to me,' she added.

'No worries,' he said easily. 'Do you know what you want to buy?'

'Haven't a clue,' she admitted.

'Well, we'll be passing a very good garden centre in a mile or so, and they've got splendid little gifts.' He smiled faintly. 'Beryl will very much appreciate a bottle of dry sherry, so don't worry about her. There's plenty of the stuff at home and you can have one of our bottles. And I'm sure you'll see something for Pat.'

Stopping at the garden centre, a very pretty hand-painted ceramic watering can, mainly for indoor plants, was decided upon and, as the assistant wrapped it carefully in tissue, Fleur looked up at Sebastian. 'If Pat never actually uses this, it'll look lovely as an ornament, won't it?' she said.

'Oh, she'll use it,' he said. 'Pat likes nice things around her. She's a wizard with anything that grows. And she'll like it especially because you've given it to her.'

As they neared Pengarroth Hall, Fleur suddenly thought of something else she'd forgotten! To tell him of the non-existent phone call asking her to come back early… She'd been so enjoying herself, it had completely slipped her mind. It would seem odd to mention it now, she thought. Never mind—she'd invent the message for later on, when she and Sebastian had been apart for a while.

When they got home, Pat was already back in harness in the kitchen and, after staying around for a few minutes to make enquiries about Beryl, Fleur went upstairs to her room. She realized that she was feeling quite tired and, with the last of the daylight filtering in through the curtains, she lay down on the bed and closed her eyes. Just for a few minutes, she thought. Well, she was on holiday, wasn't she, and being lazy was allowed.

It was the ringing of the doorbell which woke her a whole two hours later, she saw, as she glanced at the bedside clock. It was pitch-black outside and she'd been asleep for two hours! She hadn't heard that bell since the arrival of Mia's friends on Christmas Eve. Not many visitors came to Pengarroth Hall, obviously.

She jumped out of bed quickly, deciding that today she'd have a long, leisurely bath rather than a shower.

For a full half hour she luxuriated thoughtfully in the expensive bubbles. She'd had quite long enough to make up her mind that she was definitely going home the day after tomorrow. She did not want the feelings she had about her host to trouble her common sense for a moment longer… She needed to get back to work! But first, if Beryl really was well enough to receive visitors, she'd go up to their cottage for afternoon tea tomorrow, as they'd arranged. Pat had reminded her about it when they'd come back earlier. But after that, it would be Goodbye Pengarroth Hall!

Fleur smiled to herself as she brushed out her freshly-shampooed hair in long sweeping strokes, feeling bright and light-hearted. Apart from last night's ridiculous episode, she'd slept brilliantly the whole time she'd been here, and eaten even more so, thanks to the hospitality of Pat and her host. Her host! How could she ever think of Sebastian as that, now? He would have to rank as one of her friends, surely—a friend she would keep in casual contact with, and perhaps meet up with once a year—or once every two years! She knew the saying that 'absence makes the heart grow fonder', but she also knew that absence from anyone, or anything, would eventually dull the appetite to the point where it was no longer important, no longer needed. And that was exactly what must happen here. She liked Sebastian, a lot—she may even have fallen in love with him, just a little, she acknowledged ruefully—but she was also too wary of his type to endanger her future. Her future was already mapped out. And it did not include the Sebastian Conways of this world.

As this was to be her penultimate evening here, she decided to make an effort in the dress department, choosing the only skirt she'd brought with her—a three-quarter length swirly number in midnight-blue. It went perfectly with her fine, loose pearly top, especially when she pulled her hair back into a French pleat. She looked at herself in the mirror, hoping that she hadn't overdone it, because she knew it was a glamorous ensemble. Then she shrugged. So what? Anyway, it was too much trouble to take it all off and jump into yet another pair of trousers—either her own or Mia's. Have the courage to stick to your first decisions, she told herself. Stop dithering.

Faintly in the distance she'd heard voices and as she came down the wide staircase she saw Sebastian standing in the hall talking to another man. Fleur hesitated for a second, wondering whether to turn and go back to her room, or to go on down and be introduced to the newcomer. She didn't have long to make up her mind, because both men looked up and watched her descend gracefully. It was the expression on Sebastian's face that made her catch her breath, and he came forward at once.

'Ah, Fleur...meet an old friend of mine, Rudolph Malone... We've been fairly close neighbours for yonks, haven't we, Rudy? And this...this is Fleur—one of Mia's cohorts, Rudy.'

The man came towards Fleur with his rather pale, podgy hand outstretched in greeting. 'Well, well...you never fail to surprise me, Sebastian,' he said. 'Where did you find this one, may I ask? You must let me know your source of supply!'

He was rather a short individual, Fleur noted, with indeterminate brown hair and a face which was dominated by rather thick lips. She supposed that he wasn't that bad-looking but, comparing him to the god-like Sebastian, he didn't have much of a chance. She let him hold her hand for longer than was necessary, before pulling away and smiling up uncertainly.

'I told you, *I* didn't find Fleur—she's a friend of Mia's. And staying for a short holiday before she heads back to London and a very exacting position in the field of medical research,' Sebastian replied.

'Well, well,' Rudy said again. 'How convenient that *you* happen to be here as well, old chap. You said that Mia had already returned?'

'I did. She has,' Sebastian replied, almost rudely, Fleur

thought. She saw that his expression had darkened considerably in the last few moments—perhaps this man wasn't liked here, she thought. So what was he doing here?

As if in answer to her unspoken question, Sebastian said, 'Rudy works in London too, Fleur, and he's also having a break at home.' He paused, as if regretting the next thing he was going to say. 'And, since we haven't seen each other for a couple of years—well, not to chat to anyway— he's going to stay and have supper with us this evening.'

'Aren't I the lucky one,' Rudy murmured. 'I shall insist on being allowed to sit very close to your charming visitor, Sebastian. You won't deny me, will you?'

The man hadn't taken his eyes off Fleur from the moment he'd seen her, and suddenly she felt uneasy… She'd met his slimy sort before—the sort she avoided at all costs.

Pat called from the kitchen, 'Supper's ready—I've laid up in the dining room.' Fleur knew that Pat would have been pleased to do that because she jumped at every opportunity to do things properly, and together the three of them strolled along the passageway and took their places at the table. Fleur couldn't help admiring everything—the shining cutlery and glassware, the single decorative candle and a sweet arrangement of holly leaves and berries and Christmas roses in a small bowl in the centre. Yes, Pat *would* love that watering can, Fleur thought.

The meal was delicious, marred only for Fleur by Rudy's proximity to her. He seemed gifted at being able to make their knees, their thighs, touch occasionally, and she tried not to shudder each time he did it. He hadn't waited to be asked where he should sit, but had plonked himself down on the chair next to her, half-turning so that he could look into her eyes.

'I know the sort of food that gets served up in this place,' he said, 'but the only feast I'll need is to look at my charming neighbour. That will be food enough!'

'Shut up, Rudy,' Sebastian said. 'Turn it off, for Pete's sake.' He looked over at Fleur. 'Rudy inhabits the theatrical world,' he said. 'As if you needed telling.'

Fleur wished fervently that she'd decided to dress more casually. All the daft compliments which were being thrown at her were making her feel awkward, and she hated being admired by the absurd man sitting next to her. Once or twice she caught Sebastian's eye, but the usual rather intimate look she'd become used to him sending her didn't seem to be there. He looked as uncomfortable as she was feeling, a coldness in his expression making her feel unsure of herself.

Sebastian admitted to feeling absolutely furious that he'd been more or less obliged to invite Rudolph Malone to supper. Why hadn't he just offered the man a drink and sent him on his way? Why should this lovely day have to be spoilt by an intruder—an intruder who was making one pass after another at Fleur? If he hadn't been so quick with his offer of hospitality, it needn't have happened. He speared a morsel of meat savagely with his fork. Good grief—was he *jealous*? Jealous that he was having to share Fleur with another man, even for one evening? What the hell was going on?

CHAPTER SEVEN

THE following morning, Fleur woke up later than usual. At midnight, she'd eventually excused herself but had not been able to get to sleep. Rudolph Malone's rather annoying voice—not to mention his persistent and unwelcome flattery—had stayed in her mind like a record that had become stuck in the groove. She couldn't imagine how on earth he could possibly be a friend of Sebastian's, but as they were long-time neighbours she supposed it was a social obligation to offer hospitality now and then.

She frowned briefly as she showered and got dressed. Sebastian had seemed distinctly on edge a few times during the evening…she'd noticed a look on his face that was undeniably dark and moody. After all, she thought, as she brushed out her hair and began working it quickly into one long plait, if he really disliked Rudolph Malone's company that much, why ask the man to supper? He could have made some excuse, surely? She bit her lip. She'd found Sebastian's overt coolness a touch embarrassing. It had made her feel awkward, though she wasn't really surprised, not when she thought about it. Her host was the type who didn't suffer fools gladly, and it seemed obvious to her that Rudy fell quite easily into that category. She stopped what she was doing for a moment and stared at herself in the mirror. The two men could not have been more different, she thought. Rudy was smooth-tongued, his languid gaze as he'd kept on studying her unashamedly making her cringe, his touchy-feely mannerisms distinctly offensive. While Sebastian... Well, Sebastian was something else entirely...

Then she coloured up, remembering the way his lips had found hers a couple of nights ago, the way he'd practically wrapped himself around her so closely she'd actually been aware of his heart hammering against her breast. But...had it *really* happened? Because neither of them had referred to it since, which was so incredibly odd. Then she shrugged. Who cared, anyway? She was going home tomorrow. It was time to move away, move on. With no emotional complications.

Anyway, she thought, as she went towards the door, a kiss was no big deal, surely—didn't mean a thing. She paused for a second before going down the stairs. Liar, she thought. That had been no simple kiss. Sebastian Conway—no doubt highly experienced in the art—had filled her whole body with such intense longing he could have taken her that night with no effort at all. And she felt ashamed to admit it. If she'd said yes, instead of no to him staying, what would that have done to her long-term plans? Because one-night stands were not for her, and never had been. If she and Sebastian had been lovers that night—as she'd known he'd wanted them to be—it would have been merely a passing pleasure to him. But not for her. It would have meant far more to her than that. Yes, it was certainly time to go home.

When she went into the kitchen, she was surprised to see Sebastian there. It was gone nine-thirty—he always breakfasted far earlier than this. He was sitting at the table, turning the pages of a daily newspaper casually, his mug of coffee untouched. He barely looked up as she came in.

'Morning, Sebastian,' she said brightly, glancing down to see that her place had already been laid at the table.

'Morning…er…Fleur…' he replied, almost as if he'd forgotten her name! When he did look up, his eyes were totally impassive as they met hers. 'I trust you slept well?' he said briefly.

Fleur's heart sank for a moment. This was not the same man who'd driven her to Truro, who'd bought her that delicious lunch, who'd sat with her for those few brief minutes in the cathedral and so thoughtfully handed her his handkerchief to dry her tears. This was another man, someone else, someone unknowable and mysterious—and not particularly friendly!

'Pat's gone down to the shops,' he added, without looking at her. 'She'll be back mid-morning, so she says, and then you're expected up at the cottage for tea, I believe.' He paused. 'Coffee's just been brewed, by the way.'

Fleur swallowed. What had happened to make him so cool with her? she asked herself. He was in a funny mood and it certainly wasn't her imagination. She sat down opposite him and began pouring out her drink.

'It looks as if I have to go back tomorrow, Sebastian,' she said. 'I've just received a call from the lab. There's a flap on about something that needs everyone there.' She reached for the cream. How easily that complete lie had slipped from her lips. It hadn't even made her blush. 'So my holiday is going to be cut short, I'm afraid,' she added. 'But I've had a great time, and I feel rested and fully restored.' She paused. 'I hope I haven't been too much of a nuisance.'

'Isn't that out of order,' he said abruptly, 'telling you to return early? Surely everyone needs a decent break to really unwind—especially in your particular field.' He drank from his mug. 'Can't you tell them that if you stay until next week, as you'd intended, you'll be in a better state of health so that they get their pound of flesh when you do return?'

Fleur was surprised at that. She'd have thought he'd have been delighted to see the back of her!

'Sadly, a couple of people are off sick,' she said. 'So they didn't have any option but to call in the rest of us.' Another lie, she thought. Well, wasn't it the case that one little lie led to another and another until you couldn't stop?

There was silence for a few moments while he finished what he'd been reading. Then, again without looking at her, he said, 'Well, what did you think of Rudy?'

Fleur hesitated. 'I…well, he's rather…outspoken, isn't he?' she replied slowly. She'd better be careful because the man was Sebastian's friend. It wouldn't do to express herself too freely.

'If you mean he's rather full of himself, then I would certainly go along with that,' he said flatly.

Fleur shrugged. 'He's in the theatre, so you said. I believe they're all a bit like that. Goes with the territory.'

'Did you…find him attractive?' was the next question, which caught Fleur right off guard.

She frowned briefly. 'I didn't think about him in those terms,' she said.

'Oh, come off it. All you women size us men up and down, make instant assessments, don't you?' he persisted. 'Viewing the potential candidate to progress the human race… All way back in the subconscious, of course, but I believe it to be a substantial fact.'

'I can't speak for others,' Fleur said calmly. 'I certainly didn't find him…interesting…if that answers your question.'

'Oh, well, I just thought you two were getting on rather well, that's all,' he went on. 'You seemed to be hanging on to his every word, giving him all the attention, which he was clearly lapping up. It saved me from having to entertain the man,' he added. 'You did that all by yourself.'

Right, Fleur thought. If he wanted a battle, she was up for it.

'He was a guest in the house, Sebastian,' she said coldly, 'as *I* am. And if I had thrown the evil glances at him that *you* did, I would have failed to discharge my duty in that capacity. So if you really want me to give you my honest opinion of the gentleman, here it is. I thought he was the most revolting little creep that I've met in a long time, curling his ankle around mine like some disgusting worm. Would you like me to have slapped his face, demanded an apology, and then run from the room? Well, sorry to disappoint, but I'm not combative by nature. I prefer to avoid trouble if possible. And, incidentally, it was *your* feelings that were uppermost in my mind. It would have been embarrassing for you if I'd made a scene. So, to answer your enquiry, I did not find him attractive, not one bit. And, as for that squeaky little giggle of his, I'm sure that's a condition he could get treatment for.' She paused, her face flushed. 'The man is a complete buffoon,' she finished.

He closed his newspaper with a flourish and stood up. 'I think I've got the message,' he said, 'but you acted out the part very well. So perhaps I should thank you for that. He left almost as soon as you'd gone to bed, by the way, so clearly he thought there wasn't anything else worth staying for.' He turned away to fetch his jacket from the hook. 'I'll be away for the rest of the day, so…enjoy your…last one,' he added, going out and closing the door.

When he'd gone, Fleur sat back, completely confused. What on earth was all that about? she asked herself. The man was a peculiar mixture, there was no doubt about that. Often kind and considerate…even beguiling…but today he was like a quarrelsome child. And, this morning, undeniably irritable. Perhaps he and his 'friend' had drunk too much last night. Perhaps that was it. There was no other reason that she could think of. Then she made a face to herself. Let him get on with it. This time tomorrow she'd be well out of here.

Pat returned later on in the morning and Fleur was really pleased to see her, to see her open, friendly, uncomplicated face. Sebastian's attitude earlier had upset her more than she wanted to admit, and it was comforting to have the older woman around.

'I'm roasting a little duckling for tonight, for you and Sebastian,' Pat said. 'He's very partial to game, so that'll please him.'

'Hmm,' Fleur said non-committally. The fact was, Sebastian Conway had always been a spoiled brat, she thought. Brought up to expect the best of everything, and getting it, thanks to his heritage.

'Are you happy enough with bread and cheese and some soup, now, Fleur?' Pat asked, 'or do you fancy something else?'

'Bread and cheese will be absolutely perfect, thanks, Pat,' Fleur replied, smiling at the woman gratefully. She paused. 'I'm going to miss you terribly when I go home tomorrow…'

'Oh, but you're not going until next week, are you?' Pat said, turning to look at Fleur, her face crestfallen.

'Sorry—no, I've got to go back early,' Fleur replied. 'Duty calls. But—' she smiled '—I've had the most super time, and most of it is thanks to you. You've treated me like one of the family, like a queen in fact, and my own cooking is going to seem pretty ordinary after yours.'

'Well, well, that's a disappointment,' Pat said. 'It's been lovely having you around, Fleur. Makes such a difference being with another woman, someone young to chat to.' She sighed. 'Mum and I do all right, and we love our lives here, but it can be lonely, and the best times are when the family are here, and bring their guests. Then the place comes alive. Still—' she turned back to what she'd been doing '—we mustn't grumble. We feel very privileged to work at Pengarroth Hall.'

Presently, they sat together at the kitchen table enjoying the lunch—a simple meal which, in Pat's hands, seemed to turn into a banquet. Especially as it began with a piping hot bowl of homemade curried parsnip soup.

'I hope I've left enough room for the duckling,' Fleur said, sitting back.

'Mum's making some lovely saffron buns and a potato cake for our tea first!' Pat exclaimed. 'She's so looking forward to you coming up to the cottage.'

Fleur groaned inwardly. She'd momentarily forgotten about the afternoon tea appointment! But, if it killed her, she'd eat some of Beryl's home-made cakes!

At three o'clock, with Pat leading the way along the wooded paths, they went up to the cottage and Fleur was surprised at how soon they arrived. 'It doesn't take you too long then, Pat, to come down to the house?' she asked. 'Which is just as well, seeing you have to do it so frequently.'

'Oh, my, no, dear,' Pat said. 'Doesn't take any time at

all, especially when you know the way, like I do. It takes Mum a bit longer, but then, she only comes to the house when I need a bit of extra help. There are other cottages on the estate, which are rented out, but ours is the nearest—for obvious reasons.'

As they pushed open the door, the smell of fresh baking greeted them and Fleur sniffed the air like a hungry child. 'Oh…I wish I hadn't eaten so much lunch, Pat!'

The woman grinned, calling up the narrow staircase, 'Mum? We've arrived. Are you decent?' She turned to Fleur. 'Mum has a rest after lunch every day.'

'Of course,' Fleur said. 'Is she really all right, Pat—to have me up here, I mean… Has she recovered?'

'Perfectly,' Pat assured her. 'She gets these funny turns fairly regularly, but they soon pass. And she's been looking forward to your visit—insisted on baking the cakes. I could have done it, but no, she's the one in charge here.'

Just then Beryl appeared, wearing a pretty pink jumper and navy skirt, with her almost-white hair brushed up into a knot.

'You look nice, Beryl,' Fleur said.

'Well, we don't often have visitors,' the woman replied. 'Now, let me have your jacket and scarf and you sit there—kettle's already boiled.'

The modest-sized room was simply furnished but cosy and immaculate, the small dining table laid with a white lace cloth and rose-patterned china. Fleur leaned back and looked around her admiringly. 'This is the sort of room you'd see in a child's picture book,' she said, looking up at Beryl. 'So…appealing…and lovely.'

'Old fashioned, you mean,' Pat said good-naturedly. 'But it's how we like it, don't we, Mum?'

Beryl poured boiling water into the pot, then brought the

plates of cakes over to the table. 'Now, dear, have you ever tasted potato cake—the real thing, I mean? Like we make down this way?'

Fleur studied the plate she was being shown, on which was a rather flat-shaped cake, criss-crossed on the slightly browned top and dusted with sugar. 'I don't think so,' she replied, her mouth already watering. 'How's it made, Beryl?'

'Easy,' Beryl said. 'Cooked, mashed potatoes, big spoonful of fresh beef suet and the same of sugar, all mixed up by hand, add a few currants, shape it up on a baking sheet, mark it out so it's easy to serve, and let it cook slowly for about an hour. Eat it hot. Like this.' And, with the deft use of a sharp knife, she lifted a generous piece onto Fleur's plate and stood back. 'Try it,' she said.

Fleur did—and it was delicious. Her obvious enjoyment naturally pleased Beryl, and for the next half an hour all three women tucked into it, their teacups being refilled regularly.

'Now, how about a saffron bun—have you ever had saffron buns?' Beryl said, really getting into entertainment mode, but Fleur shook her head regretfully.

'Honestly, Beryl, I've had three slices of potato cake! I couldn't eat another mouthful!'

'Well, have a rest and come back in a minute,' Beryl said happily. 'I've looked out those two books we were talking about the other day, by the way.'

'Oh, I don't think I'll be here long enough to read them,' Fleur said. 'I'm going home tomorrow, Beryl—a bit earlier than I originally thought.'

'Well, take them with you, dear, and you can bring them back next time you're here.'

There won't be a next time, Fleur thought, but instead she said, 'I can't thank you both enough for all you've done to make me so welcome…I've never had a holiday like this, and I've loved every minute of it.' Bending down, she reached for her bag and took out the tissue-wrapped bottle of sherry which Sebastian had left out for her. 'This is just a little thank you, Beryl—and don't drink it all at once!'

'Oh, my goodness—thank you so much,' the woman replied, 'but you shouldn't have, you know. You've been a rather special guest—it's been a pleasure to look after you. Not that I've done much, but I know *Pat's* enjoyed your company.' She hesitated, then added rather slyly, 'To say nothing of our lord and master.'

Fleur looked away at that, then reached for her gift for Pat. 'And I hope you'll find a use for this, Pat.'

Pat unwrapped the watering can, holding it up to admire it. 'It…it's beautiful, Fleur,' she said. She paused. 'Of course I'll use it. And I shall always treasure it.'

No one spoke for a few minutes after that, and Fleur wondered whether it was time to go back.

'You've done Sebastian the world of good, Fleur. We've not seen him so…so relaxed in a long time,' Pat said, breaking the silence. 'And both Mum and I think that it's because *you're* here. He obviously likes you a lot and it's good to see him happy again—especially after what happened.'

Fleur had coloured up at the words, but admitted to being curious as to what Pat was talking about. 'What did happen?' she asked.

'Oh, don't you know—hasn't Mia told you?'

'Told me what?'

'Well, Sebastian was going to be married to one of Mia's friends—well, actually, Mia hadn't known her for that long but she introduced her to Sebastian and he fell for her. Hook, line and sinker. He never tended to bring girlfriends down here—though he had plenty of them, I believe, and he was considered a bit of a playboy when he was younger. Anyway, we all got excited when this one turned up—Davina, her name was. She looked like something out of a fashion magazine—and actually I quite liked her. She was friendly enough. But obviously something pretty disastrous must have happened because, out of the blue, they finished, everything was cancelled. And, after that, Sebastian didn't come home for a while—he left everything here for Frank and the others to deal with. Most unlike him. Anyway, it became a taboo subject very quickly and no one ever refers to it now. But Mum and I think it's high time he found someone else—and we think that you'd be just the one for him, Fleur.' She sat back with the satisfied air of someone who had just made a profound and world-changing statement.

Fleur gave a slightly hysterical giggle and covered her mouth with her hand. 'You must be joking!' she exclaimed. 'My goodness, Sebastian has been a very kind host, I can't deny that, but I assure you that's all he is. I know neither of us is looking for a relationship…I'm very dedicated to my work…but though I'm flattered that you place me in the elevated position as a possible partner for him, I don't think he would share your enthusiasm. In fact, I'm sure he wouldn't,' she added, remembering the morning's conversation.

'Well, that's where you're wrong,' Pat said flatly. 'I know the bloke, have known him all his life, and I've seen the way he looks at you.' She shook her head briefly. 'Mum and I have been chatting and we think it would be fantastic if you could bring him out of his shell again, bring him back to how he used to be. When that woman departed—whatever the reason was—it took the life right out of him.' She shrugged. 'Anyway, we can't do anything about it, but we just wanted you to know what *we* think. We think he's fallen in love with you, and that's all there is to it. And it would be wonderful for Pengarroth Hall to have someone like you around permanently.'

Fleur smiled at the two women. 'Beryl—Pat—you've been reading too many of those romantic novels,' she said. 'Life—real life—isn't like that. Sebastian and I only met a few weeks ago; he doesn't know me, and I don't know him. But thank you for all the nice things you've said—and I'm sure that someone will eventually be the right one for him. It's just not me, I'm afraid.'

No more was said after that and presently, after Fleur had thanked Beryl again for her hospitality, she and Pat made their way back down to the house so that Pat could prepare the evening meal.

'I hope you don't think we spoke out of turn, Fleur,' Pat said as they reached the house. 'You know—about you and Sebastian…what we were hoping…'

Fleur smiled quickly. 'Of course I don't, Pat,' she said. 'I thought it was rather sweet of you to be so concerned for Sebastian's well-being. He's…very lucky to have such concerned friends. And he *will* meet someone soon, I'm sure. Just give him time.'

As Sebastian showered and changed in time for supper, he felt angry with himself, at his undeniable disappointment that Fleur was going home tomorrow. He'd planned one or two things they could do, places he could show her, because she was such an easy woman to please. When Mia had asked him to 'look after' her, he hadn't realized how much he was going to enjoy it!

He put on light trousers and a black open-neck shirt and brushed out his thick hair vigorously, wondering how *she* would be looking this evening. Then he stopped what he was doing, his expression closing in. They'd had quite a spat this morning, and he knew it was all his fault. Unable to stop himself, he'd done it deliberately. Because he'd known very well that she had not found Rudolph Malone attractive. He was beginning to know her well enough to sense what she was feeling. And she had behaved impeccably—naturally. He wouldn't have expected anything less.

No, what had disturbed him that morning when he'd awoken, had been the memory of how she'd looked as she'd stood, poised, at the head of the stairs, coming down to meet Rudy. She had not taken the trouble to dress herself up like that before and, far from admiring her spectacular appearance, he had been filled with an unexpected dread. Because it was so reminiscent of how Davina had always put in an appearance. Asking to be admired, to be the centre of attention. And this did not fit Fleur's personality one bit. He knew that very well—yet he could not rid himself of the sense of distaste he'd experienced in seeing her like that. It was an unpleasant sense of déjà vu that he could have done without.

Then he shook himself angrily. She was going home tomorrow and a good thing too. He had his life to get on with.

CHAPTER EIGHT

AT ABOUT eleven o'clock the next morning, Fleur made her final preparations to go home. Sebastian had already left the house, but not before wishing her a casual goodbye and a safe journey, adding a slightly non-committal invitation to come and visit again some time. He had already brought her car around to the front entrance, and put her case in the boot.

Now, she gave one last look around the bedroom to make sure that she'd not left anything behind, then zipped up her hand luggage, slung her bag over her shoulder and went downstairs. Pat was in the kitchen and Fleur was aware of the tangibly sad atmosphere which prevailed. She bent down to smooth the head of the sleeping dog.

'I shall miss you, Benson,' she said softly. 'Even if you did disobey me the other day.'

'Not as much as we're going to miss *you*,' Pat sniffed.

They made their final goodbyes, with Fleur making vague promises to come back to Pengarroth Hall some time in the near future—though she knew that that was not likely to happen. She felt in her bones that her time here should have a final line drawn under it, and that now she should get back to the safety of work.

She smiled faintly as she passed the big gate at the top

end of the estate—the one she'd mistaken for the main entrance, remembering Sebastian's reaction when he'd spotted her sitting there in the semi-darkness. And, automatically, her mind did a rerun of everything that had happened since and her smile deepened. She had had a great time, as she'd told them all, but she finally admitted that the towering influence over the holiday had been that of her reluctant host.

Pausing for a moment at the crossroads before joining the B road which would eventually lead her to the motorway, Fleur made a face to herself as she thought about Sebastian. He hadn't been reluctant at all, she decided, or, if he had been, he'd covered it up very well, because after his initial antipathy to Mia's request that he should look after Fleur, he appeared to have warmed to the task with every day that had passed. If he'd wanted to avoid her, he could have done it easily enough. And, although she had deliberately tried to shut out of her mind all the things which Pat had said yesterday, the woman's remarks would keep floating back into her consciousness. To imagine, even for a second, that Sebastian fancied her was too ridiculous for words! He was clearly not looking for another emotional relationship—he'd made that abundantly clear during one of their early minor discussions on the subject, and, even if he was, there'd be a plentiful selection of women in the elevated life he led from which to choose. *She* would not be top of his list, that was for sure. Then, having hardened those thoughts in her mind, Fleur experienced the familiar tingle of sensuousness when she remembered what had happened a few nights ago in her bedroom…how she'd clung to him and, more importantly, how he'd responded. *Did* he fancy her? Or had that been the automatic, passing reaction which any red-blooded male might have made in those circumstances? She shrugged. It was difficult to tell but, anyway, it was too late now. That incident had passed like water under a bridge, and neither of them had alluded to it since.

As she drove swiftly along the smooth, well-maintained road, her mind flipped to the time they'd spent together in Truro. They had both enjoyed their time together there—*she* had certainly enjoyed experiencing the city and then, when he'd joined her in the cathedral, his attitude had been so...so special. It had been a simple, yet magical day and he had been so considerate, so warm, and there seemed to have been that certain thread of familiarity between them which only a couple—a devoted couple—might expect to enjoy.

Irritated with herself for dwelling on things—things which were now of the past—she put on a CD and let the music of one of the Verdi operas swell around her like a comforting tide, filling her mind with its beauty.

The traffic began to thicken as she sped along, hampered largely by various delivery trucks and milk and petrol tankers, but as the distance between herself and Pengarroth Hall—and its owner—lengthened, Fleur felt distinct relief, a lightening of her mood. She was glad she'd decided to invent the excuse to go home early—because, right there in the centre of all her other thoughts, was the uncomfortable memory of Sebastian's behaviour yesterday morning at breakfast. His suggestion that she had given Rudolph Malone undue attention, or that she had been making up to him, had upset her more than she wanted to admit. It was an offensive, preposterous suggestion, but it was Sebastian's manner which had been the worst part. He had been almost aggressive—accusing—and she had given him no reason to be either.

Fleur's lips set in a tight line. That little episode had been a demonstration of the real Sebastian, she thought with a trace of bitterness. He had obviously felt an unusual lack of control in that particular scenario, and he hadn't liked it. She shrugged. Well, was she surprised? He fitted perfectly into the mould of men to avoid.

Working up in the top fields with Frank as they stood listing and marking the trees needing attention, Sebastian felt moody and annoyed with himself. He'd deliberately left the house early because he hadn't wanted to stand there in the drive and wave goodbye to Fleur. And he just didn't understand that, didn't understand himself. Didn't understand the minor agony he was going through.

She was just another female. Yes, she was gorgeous to look at, but he'd met plenty like that, and yes, she was highly intelligent, but his law firm had its fair share of bright females. So what was the big problem? The problem was that he felt thwarted. He had expected her—wanted her—to be staying for several more days and instead she'd gone with barely twenty four hours' notice. It had seemed to him an unduly hasty departure. Especially as he'd made plans to entertain her—as Mia had asked him to—and he'd looked forward to it. He knew he was being petty-minded and he could kick himself for his feelings, his folly. But, unfortunately for him, he'd been drawn to Fleur—drawn to her like a pin to a magnet—from almost the first moment he'd set eyes on her. He knew he should resist these impulses, because it was safer, in his own best interests to remain emotionally unshackled...wasn't it? So why wasn't he pleased that she'd gone? He kicked idly at a clod of earth beneath his boot. The damnable thing was that he knew she wasn't in the least interested in *him*—and that only fired his longing to have her, to have his own way. He knew it to be one of the frailties—or strengths—of his character that when anything was denied him he didn't rest until he'd succeeded in getting it. And now she'd gone and he somehow didn't think it would be easy to entice her back to Pengarroth Hall.

'So what do you reckon about this one then, Sebastian?' Frank asked for the third time, and Sebastian looked back at the man quickly.

'Sorry, Frank—what did you say?'

'This one.' Frank tapped a tree trunk with his stick. 'I think it should probably come down.'

'Yes. Yes, I agree,' Sebastian said vaguely, and the older man stared at him, his shrewd eyes narrowing slightly.

'What the 'ell were you thinking about just then?' he asked. 'You were miles away.'

'Um…sorry, Frank,' Sebastian muttered, thinking that he'd been about fifty miles away, which was where she'd be by now.

Much later, back at home, Fleur made herself a large mug of tea and started to unpack. As she pulled everything out of her case, she realized that she'd brought one of Mia's tracksuit pants with her by mistake. She shrugged—it didn't matter because she'd be sure to meet up with her friend again soon. And Mia would expect a blow-by-blow account of everything she'd done at Pengarroth Hall. She paused for a second, her mind going backwards again. One thing she would *not* be describing was her ghostly nightmare. She must try and pretend that had never happened—and she was certain that Sebastian would never bring the subject up. Least said, soonest mended, she thought.

As she took the last of her things from the case, she suddenly spotted Sebastian's handkerchief—the one he'd so thoughtfully passed to her in the cathedral—nestling in amongst her tights. What was it doing there? And why hadn't she given it back to him straight away, or given it to Pat to go into the laundry? She bit her lip. Well, she'd give that to Mia as well, when she saw her, she thought. There'd be no need for any explanations. But, as she picked up the handkerchief, she held it to her nose for a second. It could only belong to Sebastian, she thought... It had his distinctive smell—a mixture of aftershave or cologne and the pervasive fresh, sweet scent of country air and leaves and bracken. She stared across to her window, where the only sight she could see was the tall brick wall of the building next door... *Why* had she come home early? she thought. She could still be there in Cornwall, she and Benson could go for a gentle stroll before she sat down with Sebastian to one of Pat's mouth-watering meals! No regrets, she told herself crossly. She'd made the right decision.

She switched on the television to distract herself, then stood back and looked around her with some distaste. The flat needed a good clean, she thought. It was time to roll up her sleeves and get stuck in. Energetic housework had been the time-honoured way she'd found usually lifted her from any feelings of ennui. She had to confess that for several weeks before Christmas when they'd been so busy at work, and had then gone on to one or two festive gatherings afterwards, she'd not spent much time at home at all. Certainly not enough to move furniture about and do some cleaning and polishing. Counting the weekend, she still had six days left before her holiday was finally over, so that ought to be long enough to bring the place back up to standard. She'd begin tomorrow.

She was about to unwrap the small packet of ham she'd bought for her supper from the deli nearby when the phone rang. It was Mia.

'What are you doing at home?' Mia demanded 'You should still be on holiday!'

Fleur hesitated for only a second… She just could not go on with this deception, not with her friend, anyway. Although she *would* have to manipulate the truth, just a tad.

'Oh hi, Mia. How…how did you know I was back?' she asked—but thinking that there could only be one answer to that.

'I rang home to talk to you, and was told by Pat that you'd been called back to work. Honestly, what a pain.'

Fleur took a deep breath. 'Mia—look, I'll come clean. The lab hasn't been in touch at all. It was just that I thought…I got the impression that…'

'What? Don't tell me Sebastian was being difficult…'

'Oh, no, no, of course not,' Fleur replied quickly, 'but I did think that I might be outstaying my welcome. He's very, very busy with everything, and I began to think I was in the way…' The words petered out as she tried to give a rational explanation. 'And Pat has put in so much effort on my behalf—I've never eaten meals like it in my life.' She patted her waistline as she spoke. 'But it was a wonderful break, Mia, thanks your kind offer that I should stay, and I felt so well the whole time. In fact, I've had to keep re-minding myself to take those tablets.'

'I think you were probably over-sensitive, Fleur, because Pat couldn't stop going on about how much she liked you,'

Mia said. 'Now, tell me everything. I hope Sebastian showed you around the area, took you one or two places…'

'Sebastian was extremely kind,' Fleur began carefully, sitting on the arm of her sofa and preparing herself for a long discourse. Mia liked all the details in Technicolor.

After making plans to meet up next week, they were about to ring off when Fleur said casually, 'By the way, Mia, don't tell Sebastian, you know, that I came back because I felt in the way… It's best that he thinks I'm indispensable at work.'

'OK,' Mia replied cheerfully, though thinking that she'd jolly well find out what her brother had said, or done, to give Fleur the impression she was in the way.

Much later, curled up comfortably in her dressing gown, Fleur rang her parents. Philip answered the phone and his pleasure on hearing his daughter's voice was tangible.

'*Hello* there, Fleur! Well, my word, you *are* having a good break, aren't you, dear? All raring to go back to work, I expect? What? Oh, yes, Mum and I are fine, enjoyed Boston, but it's good to be back in harness. Holidays are fine but too much of it addles the brain.'

Fleur let him go on, interspersing everything he had to say with casual remarks of her own about Cornwall. 'Is Mum there?' she asked.

'No, she's gone next door. New grandchild staying there, I believe.' He sighed, clearly mystified as to why anyone should be interested in babies. 'When she's stopped drooling, I'll get her to ring you, OK? Thanks for the call, and all the best. Let's hope for a successful year for all of us.'

Fleur snapped the phone shut, smiling faintly. Dad'll never change, she thought—and anyway, would she really want him to? At least he was consistent—and he was never unkind. Everyone had their faults, but no one was all bad, she mused.

She decided to go to bed. She'd had a lengthy drive and the day had seemed incredibly long. Snuggling under her duvet, she lay there staring up at the ceiling for a moment... It felt quite strange to be back home amongst her own things and she realized how quickly she'd settled into Pengarroth Hall—she'd felt at home there straight away. She wondered whether Pat was still there, or whether she'd returned to her cottage to be with Beryl. That potato cake had been absolutely scrummy, Fleur thought sleepily—she'd have a go at doing that herself one of these days. What was the recipe again...flour and suet and sugar and...?'

With a start, she was brought back from almost-sleep by the ringing of her phone and she sat up quickly. Glancing at the clock, she saw that it was eleven o'clock and she frowned—her mother wouldn't ring at this hour because Philip always said that telephone calls from, or to, anyone should cease after nine p.m., other than in emergencies.

'Hello?' she said sleepily—and the voice that answered sent a rush of pleasure right through her.

'Oh, good—you're home, safe and sound,' Sebastian said. 'Good journey?'

'No problems to speak of,' Fleur replied, smiling. It was so good to hear him.

'I haven't disturbed you, have I?' he said. 'You weren't asleep?'

'No,' she replied truthfully, 'I wasn't asleep—though I am in bed.'

There was a pause after that, and Fleur imagined him lounging there alone, probably in the sitting room, fingering a glass of red wine or a whisky. And Sebastian pictured Fleur's graceful, feminine curves as she lay in bed, pictured her hair spread out on the pillow, imagined the creamy smoothness of her skin.

He cleared his throat. 'Actually, I've been talking to my sister, so I knew you were home,' he went on. He would like to have said that he'd wanted to hear her voice—but didn't think that was a good idea. 'But I thought I'd ring anyway,' he added.

'I'm glad you did, because now I can thank you again for my holiday, Sebastian,' Fleur said. 'I...I did love every minute of it.' Well, not quite every minute, she thought, but most of them. 'I think Pengarroth Hall and the surroundings are just...idyllic,' she went on, 'and if I were in your shoes, I'd be counting the days before living there permanently.'

He ignored that last remark because it only reminded him of the distance which would soon separate him from the city life he enjoyed, from the people he was close to... And from any chance he might have found to spend time with this woman—a woman who had slipped so effortlessly into his life and to such significant effect! He still had difficulty in believing it because *vulnerable* was not a word he'd ever use to describe himself.

'Oh, we were happy to have you stay...Pat's gone into a sulk because it's only me here now.' He paused. 'And you don't need to thank me—it was all Mia's idea, anyway.'

Fleur froze at that last remark, feeling an uncomfortable chill run through her. Yes, of course it had been Mia's idea that she should prolong her holiday—plus the fact that he should spare some of his valuable time to act out the genial host. Let there not be any doubt about *that*! she thought. She bit her lip, wondering what to say after that.

'Oh, by the way, I very stupidly forgot to give you back

your handkerchief—the one you lent me when we were in Truro? I'll let Mia have it when we get together next week.'

'Oh, yes…I remember,' he said casually. 'But don't worry about it, Fleur, I've got others.'

For some unaccountable reason, neither of them wanted to be the one to hang up first, and Sebastian said seriously, 'Don't let them harass you at work, Fleur. I don't want all that rest and relaxation to be swallowed up now, and ruined by undue pressure.'

Fleur was frankly amazed at his genuine concern. Did he really care whether she was hassled or not? She swallowed and said quickly, 'No, I promise to do only my fair share, and to be sensible, not to stay on too long after hours.'

'Well, I hope you mean it,' he said firmly. It had been noticeable how well she'd begun to appear after the first day or so at Pengarroth Hall, how that winsome, wistful, rather tired look had been replaced by a healthy glow to her cheeks, by a tantalizing sparkle in her large eyes. Cornish air had obviously suited her, he thought.

She stifled a yawn. 'Well, I suppose I'd better go to sleep,' she said softly. 'I know it'll be a busy day tomorrow.' She crossed her fingers as she said it. Yes, she *would* be busy—cleaning her flat!

He paused before answering. 'Yes, of course. So…I'll be back in town myself in about ten days…and I'll be seeing Mia at some point. Perhaps we could all get together for a drink.'

'Perhaps.' Fleur smiled. 'Goodnight, then, Sebastian.'

As he rang off, Sebastian stared moodily into the dying embers of the fire. More than anything in the world at that precise moment, he wanted to be somewhere else. And he knew where that was. He wanted to be with Fleur, wanted to be holding her close to him, to mould her body to his, to possess her…fully…and all his senses rushed at him as he remembered the feel of her mouth on his when they'd kissed the other night. But he didn't think she'd given it another thought…there'd been no look, no word, not the slightest sign that it had had the impact on her that it had on him. She liked men—oh, yes, he was sure that she liked men. She just didn't want to be…how could he put it…cornered by anyone in particular. She wanted to be a beautiful *Mary Celeste*, sailing alone.

He stood up, kicking aside a footstool irritably. There was not the remotest chance that the relationship he wasn't sure he wanted would ever come to anything. The best thing for him would be to try and forget that he'd ever met Fleur. But how the devil was he going to do that?

CHAPTER NINE

IN HER kitchen on the Saturday evening ten days later, Fleur stood rather precariously on her short stepladder and started to paint the ceiling, wielding the large brush back and forth vigorously.

Having used up some of her holiday, plus more time since, in spring-cleaning the flat, she'd come to the conclusion that the kitchen had gone beyond needing a mere clean-up—it needed redecorating. And, once she'd made up her mind that that was what she was going to do, she'd lost no time in buying everything that was needed. She'd decided that this time the walls would be the palest green—which would suit the oak cabinets—with the skirtings and other woodwork gloss white. And when she'd completed the job, she thought, straining her head back and looking upwards at the rather challenging area to be done, she'd have a great time purchasing some new stuff—towels and tea towels, and maybe replacing some of her china as well. All to blend in. She felt the definite need to inject something new, something original, something to kick-start the new year.

She'd been welcomed back to work with open arms by her colleagues, who'd all said how well she looked and teased her that she'd put on weight, and soon it felt to

Fleur that Pengarroth Hall and her time there was becoming a distant memory. But lives were built on memories, she thought now, and she had so many locked away into hers…things she would never, ever forget.

Bending to dip her brush carefully into the paint pot, her thoughts were of Sebastian—as they seemed so often to be—and she was glad she'd not heard anything from him since his phone call. Time was already passing so rapidly, and it was only time which would help her to push him further and further away from her, so that he stopped being the first thing on her mind each morning when she woke and the last thought each night before going to sleep. But it wasn't just him, Sebastian Conway, she tried to convince herself. It was Pengarroth Hall and its atmosphere, it was Pat and Beryl's friendship, and the clear, melting Cornish air. As her thoughts ran on, she grimaced slightly as she remembered Rudolph Malone's visit. His appearance on the scene had been the one thing—apart from Sebastian's reaction to it—to mar the perfect holiday. Then she shrugged. Who cared, anyway? She'd never come face to face with that silly man again.

She was about three-quarters of the way through the area to be painted when the doorbell sounded, and its unexpected intrusion almost made Fleur drop the brush. She paused, frowning. Who would call on her without ringing first? she asked herself. And at nearly nine o'clock on a Saturday night? She put down the brush and began to climb down from the ladder cautiously but, before she could get to the door, the bell rang again—twice in quick succession.

'OK, OK, hang on a minute…' she called. 'I'm just coming.'

As she went into the hall, she glanced at herself in the

long mirror—heavens, what a sight she looked! She was
wearing the oversized and stained decorator's apron—an
old one of her father's—which she always used, and had
tied her hair up in a knot with a tatty scarf to keep it in place
and to protect her hair from any white splashes. The only
make-up she had on was a big smudge of ceiling white on
one cheek—which was also on her hands, she noticed,
rubbing them down the apron hurriedly.

Going forward quickly, she peered into the security
peephole—and gasped in surprise and a certain degree of
horror. *Sebastian*, she thought—*what on earth?*

She opened the door and they both stood there for a
moment without saying a word, Sebastian looking at her
up and down, a curious expression on his face.

'Oh—I've obviously come at a bad time,' he began, and
Fleur cut in at once, standing aside. Well, how could she
be offhand or unwelcoming—even if she was in no fit state
to receive guests?

'It's all right, Sebastian, come in,' she said quickly.
'Though you'll have to take me as you find me,' she added.

He entered, but stood there, just taking in her appearance for several seconds and there was absolutely nothing
Fleur could do to make herself look anything other than
grubby and unattractive. But, as he stared down at her,
Sebastian's only thought was how utterly seductive she
looked... There was something so appealing in the hastily
drawn-back hair, the untidy scarf, the careless dabs of
white on her skin. He could as easily have swept her up
into his arms and covered her mouth with kisses as on
those other times when, immaculately turned out, she had
stirred his desire. He couldn't help fleetingly remembering the time she'd stood at the top of the staircase looking

like a society darling—he knew which picture he would want to keep close to his heart.

'I won't ask you what you're up to, because I can see for myself,' he said casually, following her into the sitting room. 'I didn't realize you were a painter and decorator.'

'It's my kitchen,' she explained. 'I decided that it was some time since it had had a makeover—and a new year seems appropriate to change things a bit, don't you think?'

He was wearing well-cut trousers, a purple shirt, open at the neck, and an expensive long dark coat—and, not for the first time, Fleur found herself admiring the casual elegance which seemed to personify the man. But she was also aware of the tiny flecks of grey beginning to show a little more in his hair. Today he did look the seven years older than her, she thought impulsively.

There was a distinct sense of awkwardness between them—they both felt it—and Fleur went on hurriedly, 'So…you're obviously back in London now, Sebastian… When do you expect to return to Pengarroth Hall? And do sit down,' she added, indicating one of the armchairs. 'Can I offer you a drink—something to eat?' Help, she thought, what have I said? It wouldn't be easy to produce anything in her kitchen at the moment.

He didn't sit, but came towards her slowly and for a moment Fleur thought he was going to take her in his arms…then…

'Fleur…' The word was almost choked out, and involuntarily she put out a hand.

'What…what is it, Sebastian?'

There was a long pause while he struggled to utter the words. 'It's Benson…he died two days ago.' He waited before going on. ' We…we buried him in the grounds yesterday.'

'Oh, *no—Benson*!' Fleur covered her face in her hands, hot tears springing to her eyes. 'What...?'

'Of course, none of us should have been surprised,' Sebastian said quietly. 'He was a very old dog, but I can barely remember a time when he wasn't there. He...he seemed to be his usual self in the morning,' he went on, 'then suddenly he couldn't get up from the floor and just looked at us as if he was trying to tell us what was the matter. But, before we could even call the vet, he lay his head down on my knees and... and was gone. In a couple of minutes. At least we were all there to say goodbye.' Sebastian swallowed hard before going on. 'But it's hit us all badly—Pat's been in tears ever since, and Frank's going around with a perpetual scowl on his face.'

It was obvious that Sebastian was terribly upset—and trying hard not to sound too sentimental—and, without thinking what she was doing, Fleur went across and put her arms around his neck, burying her head in his shoulder.

'Poor, dear Benson,' she whispered. 'I wish I'd been there as well, I wish I'd been there to hold him.'

'Yes, I wish you had,' Sebastian said. 'Benson loved you, Fleur, we could all tell. That was why he wouldn't come back home with you on that walk. He wanted you to stay out there with him in the woods.'

A stifled sob left Fleur's lips at his words, and she looked up into Sebastian's face. 'That dog would never have known anything but love and comfort,' she said, 'and, from what you say, he didn't suffer, did he? Not even at the end?'

'No. We don't think so,' Sebastian replied.

'So...he was lucky, wasn't he—lucky to have all of you for his whole life. There are many animals who don't have that kind of luck.'

They stood there still locked together, and Sebastian said, 'I'm sorry to have intruded on you like this, but I just couldn't bring myself to ring you with the news...I wanted to tell you, face to face...because I knew you'd be upset, too.'

Fleur tried hard to stem her tears, and Sebastian put his hand in his pocket and gave her his handkerchief.

'Here,' he said, 'have another one. I told you I had plenty.'

In spite of everything, they both managed to smile at his words. Fleur took the handkerchief and blew her nose and wiped her eyes, sighing heavily. 'Oh, dear,' she said. 'I don't feel like doing any more painting tonight. In fact, I don't feel like doing anything at all.' She blew her nose again. 'I hate bad news,' she said.

'I know, and I'm sorry,' Sebastian said quickly, pulling her into him even more closely. 'I just wanted someone to be miserable with, and you were the first one I thought of. Sorry.'

'Is that a compliment?' Fleur asked, beginning to recover, and thinking that she'd shed more tears since knowing Sebastian than she'd allowed herself in half a lifetime. It had to be those tablets, she thought. She'd take the last few, and that would be it. It was not like her to give way so easily... She'd always been taught that undue emotion portrayed a weakness of character.

'I hope you will take it as such,' he replied. 'I haven't even told Mia yet.'

Fleur looked at him quickly. Well, it *was* a compliment, she thought, to have been put first in these circumstances, and it made her feel ridiculously important...and...special. She went over to the small cabinet in which she kept her modest supply of alcohol.

'I think we both need a drink,' she said, looking across

at him. 'I do have some whisky, Sebastian, or would you prefer wine?'

'What I'd really appreciate is a good strong cup of tea,' he said unexpectedly. 'If you can actually produce one— in the present state of your kitchen, I mean?'

Fleur smiled quickly. 'Yes, I can definitely manage a cup of tea,' she said lightly, 'and there's an unopened packet of chocolate digestives to go with it, as well. But I'd better clean myself up a bit first.'

He followed her into the kitchen and looked around him speculatively. 'Look,' he said, 'you're halfway through the ceiling—and you're making a good job of it too—it seems a shame to leave it.' He shrugged off his coat, and looked down at her. 'Let me finish it for you while you make the tea.'

'Oh, honestly, Sebastian…I don't want to put you to any trouble. I can do it tomorrow…'

'No, we'll finish it now,' he said firmly. 'It's not good to leave your post in the middle of a job. If you'll let me have the use of that somewhat roomy apron, I can do it in half an hour. And I think the tea can wait.' He grinned down at her. 'Come on, no arguments. It'll do me good to do something positive.'

Fleur understood exactly where he was coming from with that remark and, without another word, she untied the massive apron and handed it to him. 'This is certainly more your size than mine,' she said. 'And I must admit that my neck was beginning to ache, looking upwards all the time. It was taking longer than I thought it would.'

'So it's just as well that I turned up,' he said reasonably. 'It's an ill wind that blows nobody any good. Isn't that what they say?'

Fleur watched as he set to with the brush, and was impressed with how quickly he was covering the area. 'If I'd known you were going to arrive, I would have waited so that you could have done it all,' she joked.

'I should have let you know,' he said apologetically, glancing down at her briefly, 'but it was only as I was nearing town that I made up my mind to try my luck and see if you were in.' He dipped the brush into the pot again and resumed painting.

'How...how did you know where I lived, anyway?' Fleur asked curiously.

'All your details were written down on the pad in the kitchen—you obviously gave them to Pat, because they were in her handwriting,' he said casually.

'Oh, yes—of course,' Fleur said. 'I remember now. She wants us to keep in touch—which is what I want too, of course.'

In less than forty minutes the job was complete, and Sebastian surveyed his handiwork critically. 'I think that'll do,' he said, 'and if you see any bits I've missed—white on white is always difficult, especially in artificial light— I'll drop back and touch it up.' He put the lid firmly back on the pot and went across to the sink to wash the brush and, as Fleur watched him for a second, she thought how surreal it was that he should be here, painting her ceiling, when she hadn't expected to see him ever again—or, at least, not for a very long time.

He finished what he was doing and turned, looking down at her as he took off the apron. 'I've gone off the idea of tea,' he said. 'A glass of your whisky would be much appreciated—if it's still on offer.'

Fleur smiled up at him. 'Of course it is,' she said, 'and

then I'll prepare us some supper—unless you're going on somewhere?'

He shook his head briefly. 'No, I've got no plans,' he said.

'Then I'll wave my magic wand and get us something to eat—though it won't be up to Pat's standard, I'm afraid,' she said, going over to the drinks cabinet, and Sebastian sat down in the armchair with his whisky while Fleur went into the kitchen.

'I'm doing us cheese omelettes—or you could have ham,' she called. 'Which do you want?'

'Cheese will be fine,' he replied. Then, 'Can I help?'

She smiled to herself. 'No, I think I can manage this all by myself,' she said, 'but I'll let you make the coffee later.'

It was surprising how quickly they'd both managed to step back from thinking about poor, dear Benson, Fleur thought, reminding herself again how blessed routine and activity helped to dull pain—at least temporarily. It would take Sebastian—and the others—some time to come to terms with not having the lovely animal around, but at least for the moment Sebastian seemed less upset, though she had to swallow a lump in her own throat as she remembered the dog's soulful eyes looking up at her. And she couldn't help feeling an enormous sense of privilege that *she* had been chosen to be told the news. Even before Mia.

It was getting on for eleven o'clock by the time they sat down, with a tray each on their laps, and enjoyed the soft, buttery omelettes and thinly sliced brown bread.

'I think Pat would say you have done us proud,' Sebastian said as he mopped up the last of his supper with a piece of crust, then put down his knife and fork. 'That was actually quite fantastic,' he added. 'And I hadn't eaten since lunch.'

'It probably seemed fantastic because you were hungry,' Fleur said, 'and so was I.' She took his tray, then went back into the kitchen to put the kettle on. And almost at once he was by her side, standing behind her, with his hands lightly on her waist, before sliding them gently to rest on her hips—for just a moment… She had difficulty in not shivering in pleasure at his touch. Instinctively, she turned away and indicated the coffee things on the shelf.

'There you are,' she said lightly. 'Your turn.'

With the television flickering in the corner, they drank their coffee on the sofa in what Fleur could only think of as companionable ease, with neither of them feeling the need to make unnecessary conversation. Then Sebastian glanced around him.

'You have a very…cosy…place here, Fleur,' he said casually. 'It has your taste stamped all over it, if I may say so.'

Fleur smiled at that. 'I've been here for three years,' she said, 'and the first thing I did was change things as much as I could without actually knocking down walls. My father helped me decorate, but I chose everything myself. It's lovely to own something for one's self, isn't it, and not have to worry about what other people think, or want.' She paused. 'I particularly like my bedroom—it's the largest room and it looks over the park at the back. I just *have* to see grass and trees—foliage of any kind, really—because it helps me ignore the hustle and bustle and brick walls at the front. I see children playing in the park sometimes, and people walking their dogs. I can make believe that I'm in the country somewhere.' She stopped abruptly, wondering whether she should have mentioned dogs, but Sebastian nodded in agreement.

'Yes, it's amazing what a few acres of grassland can do for people. I did bring Benson back to town with me occasionally, a few years ago, but it didn't really work out. He was much happier at home.' He drank from his cup. 'And that's where he is now,' he added.

Neither spoke for a few moments after that, then Sebastian said, 'When I went into the bathroom to wash my hands, your bedroom door was open…and I agree with you. It is a lovely room, with a big window, which must act as a kind of picture frame for the view outside.' He turned his head and looked at her steadily, not bothering to add how enticing he'd found the sight of her king-size bed with the luxurious pillows and immaculate covers. In fact, he wouldn't mind sliding beneath that duvet with her now, he thought… She was wearing a sort of clingy soft grey dress which just hinted at the curvaceous figure beneath, and she'd done her hair in two bunches, which fell casually around her neck and shoulders. He shrugged inwardly. He knew there'd be no invitation from her to spend the night here, he was sure of that.

He put his empty cup down on the small table in front of them and began to get up reluctantly. 'I suppose I'd better be going,' he said, and she looked up, treating him to one of those languid eye movements which always made the muscles of his neck twitch.

'It's past midnight,' she said coolly. 'You…you're more than welcome to stay, Sebastian.'

That was the last thing he'd expected her to say, and his heart rate went up a notch! 'Um…well…my car's parked along the street and it'll only take half an hour or so to get home,' he began, and she shrugged, getting up as well.

'It's up to you. I feel I owe you bed and board—it'll be

my way of saying thank you for doing the ceiling,' she said. 'And I always have bacon and eggs for breakfast on Sundays.'

At that precise moment the telephone rang and Fleur's expression changed at once to one of immediate concern. Frowning, she looked up at Sebastian, her eyebrows raised, then went over to answer it. And, before she had chance to say anything, Mia's voice could be heard by both of them.

'Fleur? Oh, Fleur—I haven't got you out of bed, have I?'

'No, Mia—of course not… What is it? What's the matter?'

'It's Mat! We've split up—just now. Oh, Fleur, it was horrible! We had the grandmother of all rows and he's…he's…' There was the sound of much sniffing and nose-blowing '…he slammed his way out of the flat as if I had something contagious! Honestly, he is being so unreasonable! And I'm sorry to ring you at this hour, but I couldn't go to bed, go to sleep, without telling *someone*! Why does this always happen, Fleur? I'm beginning to think that I shall never have a lasting relationship with anyone, *ever*!'

In spite of her friend's obvious distress, Fleur couldn't help smiling. Mia was always exuberant—whatever the circumstances—and she knew that this time next week she and Mat would probably have made up. 'Oh dear,' she said sympathetically, 'and I thought you were getting on so well at Christmas…'

'We *were*. It was all going brilliantly, but you're right, Fleur—men always have to be in control. Although I don't usually agree with your mantra, I do now. It's what *they* want all the time; their ideas are the only ones that count…' She blew her nose loudly again, and by now Fleur had made appropriate signs to Sebastian to give him some idea what was going on. Covering the mouthpiece with her hand, she whispered, 'Shall I tell her you're here?'

He grinned and whispered back, 'Why not?'

After listening to a few more frenzied outbursts from Mia, Fleur said gently, 'Look, there's someone else you might like to talk to, Mia…Sebastian's here.'

For a moment there was dead silence, then Mia said, '*Seb's* there? What's going on? I thought he wasn't coming back to London until next week.'

'Perhaps you'd better speak to him and let him explain,' Fleur said, handing the phone over.

'Hi, Sis. What's it this time?' Sebastian's reasonable voice seemed to calm Mia down slightly as she put him in the picture, and he smiled faintly at Fleur as he listened.

After several more minutes of pouring her heart out, Mia said, 'But…why are you over at Fleur's place? Is something the matter? No one tells me *anything*!'

'Look, it's rather a long story, and I think we'd better meet up,' he began, and Mia interrupted.

'Oh, yes, please. Will you come over and have lunch at my place tomorrow? Please say you will. I can't bear Sundays on my own—and make Fleur come too… I'm desperate to see you—to see you both…'

After arrangements were made for lunch at Mia's flat tomorrow, Sebastian hung up the phone. Fleur said, 'Well, never a dull moment with your family.' She smiled, then stretched her arms above her head, yawning. 'I *must* get to bed—and it's pointless you going home now, Sebastian— if you're having lunch with Mia tomorrow—because her flat is miles away from your place, whereas it's quite convenient to get to from here. So—' she smiled up at him sleepily, turning to go into her room '—I'll give you pillows and a spare duvet in a minute, and then I'll show you how that sofa turns into a very comfortable extra bed.'

CHAPTER TEN

WHEN she woke up the following morning it took Fleur a moment to remember exactly what had happened last night... Was Sebastian really here and sleeping in her sitting room? Then she sat up quickly. Yes, it was no dream, she assured herself. He *had* turned up last night, had painted her kitchen ceiling—and spent the night on the sofa bed. Though she had not heard a sound from him after they'd wished each other goodnight.

She threw back the duvet and reached for her dressing gown, going into the bathroom. She'd better wash and get dressed quickly so that he could have a shower, she thought. There were plenty of toiletries he could make use of, but no shaving kit. Then she shrugged. That was his problem, not hers.

When she emerged from her bedroom, she was faintly astonished to see the sofa bed returned to normal and no sign of Sebastian. She stood still, looking around her as if expecting him to materialize... *Had* she dreamed it, after all? she asked herself stupidly, knowing full well that she had not. But there was not a sign of him anywhere, and no note.

Slowly, she went into the kitchen feeling suddenly dispirited. She couldn't imagine why he'd disappeared, but the emptiness she felt made her feel forlorn. Then she made a face—for heaven's sake, don't let the man get to you like this, she scolded herself. He'd obviously had a good reason to leave the flat, but so what? She'd go on to Mia's by herself, and whether he turned up or not didn't matter. She glanced up at the ceiling—it did look great, even in the rather poor wintry light coming in the window and, as far as she could see, no spot had been missed. So he needn't bother to come back to do any patching up.

Just then, she heard her front door open and close and, going out quickly into the hallway, she saw Sebastian standing there, two large paper bags in his hand.

'Good morning, Fleur,' he said, looking down at her quizzically. 'Found your house keys on the hall table to let myself back in, in case you still hadn't surfaced, and thought if *I* didn't do something about breakfast, we'd never get to Mia's place.' He went past her into the kitchen, put the things on a shelf and switched on the kettle. 'I know you said you always cook bacon and eggs on Sundays, but I thought there wouldn't be enough time today...so I've bought hot croissants and fresh rolls instead. That's a super deli you've got next door, by the way.'

Fleur felt a rush of pleasure seep through her that he hadn't gone off somewhere without saying anything. She hadn't really thought he would be that rude, but he was something of an unknown quantity and she didn't know him well enough to be sure. She gazed up at him. There was dark stubble on his unshaven features, which might have given him a slightly menacing appearance—until she remembered his reaction at losing Benson. Whatever else he might be, he was not menacing. She smiled quickly.

'I'm sorry I woke up so late—and thanks for getting the

breakfast,' she said. 'Besides, Mia's lunches are always very generous so we'd better get there with an appetite.'

'Just what I thought,' he replied, pouring the water onto the coffee grounds in the percolator and reaching for two mugs. He glanced upwards briefly. 'Ceiling's OK,' he said. 'I don't think I missed any bits.'

'The ceiling's perfect,' Fleur said. She paused. 'I didn't want to ask Dad to help me this time… I wanted to do it by myself. But I'm really glad *you* turned up.' She stopped herself from saying any more… This wasn't good, she thought. They were getting too close and she knew that neither of them would appreciate it.

While Sebastian went into the bathroom to shower and freshen up, Fleur busied herself with putting out plates and butter, and they were soon seated once again in the sitting room, munching away at the deliciously fresh food he had bought.

'Did you manage to sleep all right?' she asked, leaning forward to refill their mugs. 'Everyone who's spent a night on that sofa bed declares it to be very comfortable.'

He looked across at her as she spoke. She was wearing well-fitting white trousers and a black figure-hugging jumper, her hair tied back in a ponytail. She had hardly any make-up on, her skin exhibiting that healthy glow he'd come to admire so much, and had put on a pair of white gold hoop earrings which dangled prettily and caught the light as she moved.

He cleared his throat. 'You don't need to apologize for the sofa bed,' he said easily. 'I slept like a log, and it has my full recommendation.' He was going to add that he hoped he'd be invited to use it again, but that wasn't what he meant. To hell with the sofa bed—he'd like to try the king-size in her bedroom, he thought. Preferably with her in it. His expression darkened briefly. Mia had warned him that Fleur was not one for emotional relationships—and Fleur had confirmed it herself. And neither was she the sort to indulge in passionate short-lived flings, either. Any plan he might have had in that direction seemed hopeless.

He stared thoughtfully into his coffee mug. He had thought he'd found the one for him when he'd met Davina—and he'd been proved horribly wrong. Yet his feelings for Fleur were on another planet entirely, and he wanted to kick himself. It was just that she was someone he wanted to be with—all the time. Not only because she was so enticingly beautiful but because she was so…so… ordinary. No, not ordinary. She was unspoilt, uncomplicated, unsophisticated, undemanding. The sort of woman he'd dreamed of finding, who might one day agree to share his life at Pengarroth Hall. But he knew that was an impossible thought. She was not the marrying kind, and certainly didn't want children. He shrugged inwardly. He knew plenty of women whom he could easily persuade to be his wife—but he didn't want any of them. He wanted just one—the one who obviously didn't want him.

The Sunday morning traffic was blissfully light and it only took half an hour to reach Mia's flat. Sebastian was able to park the car right outside, and Fleur was surprised at that—until Sebastian explained.

'Mia always arranges to park her car somewhere else,' he said, 'when she knows I'm coming—which is thoughtful of her. Otherwise we might have had a fair walk.'

Fleur had been to the imposing building several times before, but it never failed to impress her. The marble-pillared entrance announced the grandeur of what would once have been the residence of a wealthy family, but which had been turned into four spacious flats. She knew that the whole place was owned by the Conway estate, with Mia living in one of the flats and the others rented out—mostly to friends or acquaintances.

Sebastian gave a quick ring on the bell before opening the door with his own key, then ushered Fleur in front of him as they made their way along the wide, richly carpeted hallway. The discreet chandeliers above their heads threw a welcoming light as they went up the stairs and, before they could reach Mia's door, she appeared, leaning over the gleaming mahogany banister to greet them.

'Oh, good—you've timed it just right,' she enthused. 'I'm *so* glad to see you both.'

Despite her distress of the night before, Mia seemed to have recovered enough to be her usual bubbly self and Fleur thought—not for the first time—what a joy people like her were. Whatever happened, she always seemed to bounce back cheerfully.

'Now, first things first,' Mia said, as she poured some wine into three glasses and handed them around. 'What on earth were you doing at Fleur's place so late on a Saturday night, may I ask?' she demanded. 'It was only after I rang off that I realized I didn't have the faintest idea what that was all about.'

Sebastian looked sober for a moment before he spoke. 'I don't really know what I was doing there myself,' he admitted. 'But I wanted to tell Fleur something…something which I knew would upset her, and I didn't want to use the phone.'

Mia was mystified. 'Well,' she said impatiently, 'what was it?'

'Benson died a couple of days ago, Mia,' he began, 'and…'

'Oh, *no*!' Mia was aghast at the news 'What happened… how…did he go?'

'Very peacefully,' Sebastian said slowly, 'with his head in my lap. He was just tired, that's all. There was no pain.'

There were a few moments' silence while Mia absorbed the news.

'Of course, I wanted you to know too,' Sebastian went on quickly, 'but because Fleur had been at the house for some time, Benson had got used to her being there—she did make a lot of fuss of him and he liked that. They'd become firm friends, I think, and it seemed right that I should tell her face to face.' He paused. 'They had quite a relationship going in the end.'

For once, Mia seemed deflated—but it wasn't long before she recovered. 'Well…we all knew Benson's days were numbered,' she said, 'and his walks were beginning to get shorter and shorter, weren't they?' She glanced at Sebastian. 'You'll have to get a replacement, Seb. I don't think Frank— or Pat—will survive without a dog in the place.'

'There's time for that,' he replied shortly.

Fleur decided to lighten the atmosphere. 'Whatever you're cooking, Mia, it smells fantastic,' she said. 'I'm very glad I didn't cook bacon and eggs for us this morning.'

Mia was quick to pick up on that remark. 'Oh, you stayed the night, then Seb—well, well.' Her mischievous eyes twinkled as she looked from one to the other.

'I was offered the opportunity to sleep on Fleur's extremely comfortable sofa bed, to save me driving home, then having to come back again to pick her up before we came on to your place,' Sebastian explained smoothly.

'Hmm,' Mia said enigmatically, and Fleur looked across at her friend.

'I was only being polite, Mia,' she said. 'It seemed the right thing to do, especially as Sebastian had just painted my kitchen ceiling for me.'

'Painted your what?' Mia turned to Sebastian. 'I can find one or two things for you to do here if you're ever at a loose end,' she teased, 'though I don't think that any of my ceilings would have quite the appeal for you that Fleur's obviously had.'

Sebastian stood up to offer the wine around. 'Why don't we talk about you and your love life, Mia?' he said easily. 'Come on, out with it.'

'Oh, that can wait until we've eaten,' Mia said airily. 'I've cooked a piece of beef—which I would be glad if you would now come and carve please, Seb—and the roast potatoes and Yorkshire puddings are done to a turn.'

With her mouth already watering, Fleur took her place at the table and soon they were tucking into a meal which could almost have compared with Pat's.

'This is wonderful, Mia,' Fleur said, helping herself to more of the buttery carrots which Sebastian was offering around.

'Oh, I've learned everything from Pat,' Mia said. 'She's always happy to pass on her knowledge to anyone who'll listen.'

It was not until they were finishing the last of the apple tart and custard that Sebastian brought the conversation round to Mia again as he leaned back in his chair. 'Now then, what went on last night between you and your latest?' he said, and Fleur glanced at him quickly. His question sounded like that which a lawyer might ask of a client, she thought—brisk and to the point. Although the relationship between Sebastian and his sister was clearly a very loving one, she did wonder whether Mia was slightly in awe of him—especially because he was that much older than her.

'Oh, I don't know,' Mia said, pushing her plate away and leaning her elbows on the table. 'Everything was going well, and I thought that this time I'd found someone I could tolerate for the next forty years…but lately he has seemed…different…somehow. Always wants the last word. Always thinks he's right. And very determined about certain things.' She paused. 'And last night—we'd seen a good film, had supper, and then he started nagging me about something. And guess what—when I told him to go, if that's how he felt about me— he did. *Go*, I mean. Just marched out with not another word.'

'Well, if you told him to go, then it's not surprising that he did,' Sebastian said briefly. 'What else did you expect?'

Mia stared across at him. 'I did *not* expect him to go, Seb! I did not expect that at all. I expected him to stay and be reasonable. To try and see my point of view for once.'

Sebastian shrugged. 'I don't understand females,' he said. 'If a woman showed me the door, I'd be gone without a backward glance.'

'What exactly is it that you don't agree about, Mia?' Fleur asked gently. 'Is there a particular sticking point that gives rise to a lot of other silly arguments?'

Mia thought about that for a moment. 'He accuses me of being over-adventurous, of always having mad ideas…I mean…I want…I'd *love* to do a parachute jump…' She paused. 'But he's more cautious than me, and doesn't want me to do it. Says life's too short to take unnecessary risks.' She hesitated. 'I suppose you can understand it because his best friend was killed doing one a year or so ago.'

'Then you certainly *can* understand it,' Sebastian said firmly, 'and doesn't it tell you something, Mia? That the man cares enough for you that he doesn't want you to come to any harm? He *could* say, *Carry on and good luck*, but he wants you in one piece, presumably so that you can spend a lot more time together.' He shook his head as he looked across at his sister. 'When are you going to grow up and settle down, Mia? I seem to remember spending most of your teenage years—and afterwards—catching you as you fell out of trees, or into rivers.' He put his napkin down and stood up. 'Anyway, I'm with Mat, who I thought was a pretty sound bloke, by the way. I'd prefer you not to go jumping out of aeroplanes just for the fun of it. Because—' he looked down at her seriously for a second '—it's up to you to provide the next generation for Pengarroth Hall—that's the least you can do in return for all the privileges that come with the dynasty.'

Mia pretended to sulk. 'Well, *thanks* for your support, Seb. And anyway, what about you?' she said. 'Why can't *you* do something about making sure the line continues?'

'I've decided to leave that bit to you,' he said, going over to look out of the window. 'I've already planned to give up what's left of my life to run the place as efficiently as it's been done for generations. That's enough to be thinking about. The baby business is yours.'

'Well, that's all right then,' Mia said sarcastically. But it was obvious that chatting about her love life with the others had allowed her to see things in a different light. 'Anyway, Mat did ring me this morning—with a sort of apology,' she conceded. 'So I'll forgive him.' She smiled cheerfully. 'He *can* be a darling,' she said, 'and as long as he lets me win some of the arguments, I expect we'll end up together.'

'Winning half of the time is a perfectly reasonable expectation,' Sebastian said. 'Give and take. Win some, lose some. It's called being reasonable.'

He's back in lawyer mode again, Fleur thought.

Later, they sat there in the beautifully furnished room, lazily reading the Sunday newspapers.

'By the way, Mia, the law event is the Saturday after next—remember I told you about it? It's a bit earlier than usual,' Sebastian remarked.

Mia stood up to consult her calendar. 'Oh, dear, I *had* forgotten, Seb.' She ran her finger down the page. ' Sorry, but it's out of the question, I'm afraid. Big do at work. Can't possibly miss it.' She looked across at Fleur. 'But Fleur might be able to go with you…'

Fleur coloured up at the words. Mia was at it again—making arrangements for other people.

Sebastian said, '*Would* you be free on that day, Fleur? It's something I just have to attend every year and it's…useful to have a companion.'

'What he means is it helps to keep predators at bay,' Mia said, grinning. She looked down at Fleur, who was still sitting at the table. 'You'd love it, Fleur—it's always in a splendid hotel, great dinner, entertainment…and usually goodie bags for all the ladies.'

'Well, I'll have to see what…' Fleur began hesitantly, getting her diary out of her bag. Quick, make up something, she told herself—but make it sound genuine. She turned the pages of the little book—but the date was completely free. And, when she looked up, she saw that Sebastian was gazing at her with that inscrutable expression which defied any excuses she might come up with. 'I can probably go with you…' she began slowly.

'There you are, then. That's settled.' Mia beamed as she went towards the kitchen. 'I'll fill the dishwasher and Seb can make the coffee. He makes great coffee,' she said over her shoulder to Fleur.

Much later, after they'd had coffee with Mia, Fleur and Sebastian made their way back to her flat, Fleur desperately trying to find a way of saying something about the impending law dinner without sounding negative.

'Are you sure you want me to come with you to the law dinner, Sebastian?' she asked as casually as she could, gazing out of the side window. 'I'm afraid Mia has a gift for putting you in awkward situations—she's done it before, hasn't she? Aren't there lots of lovely lawyers who'd be pleased to accompany you?'

He didn't even look at her as he replied. 'There are. But I don't want them to accompany me, thanks very much. I see quite enough of them without sharing my Saturday evenings with them.' He paused at the last set of traffic lights before they reached their destination. 'I'm glad Mia suggested you come, Fleur. I can't think of anyone who'd fill the vacancy with more grace.' Now he did look at her, and his eyes were glistening darkly. 'Don't worry about it. Having to suffer my company can be a small payment for painting your ceiling.'

They pulled away again and, when they reached her flat, he turned off the engine and looked down at her. 'When do you want me to come and finish it all—the glossing, I mean? You don't want the job hanging around, do you?'

'Oh, there's no need for you to come back and do anything, Sebastian—I can manage that all right. But…thanks for the offer.' She hesitated. 'Would you like to come in for a…drink?' she asked, though thinking that *she* didn't want anything else to eat or drink until at least tomorrow.

'No, thanks, I'll be on my way,' he said. He got out of the car and came around to open her door. 'Well, have a good week—and don't overdo it, will you.'

She smiled up at him quickly. 'Thanks for your concern, Sebastian. I'm sure I'll survive whatever they throw at me.'

She watched him pull away swiftly and stood for a moment before going inside. She had very mixed feelings about her date with Sebastian…. very mixed feelings about him full stop. The thing was, she knew that she was in love with the man, but didn't want to be. Being heavily involved wasn't how she'd imagined her life to ever be. With anyone—anyone at all.

She let herself into the flat and threw her bag down on the sofa before going over to look out of her bedroom window. It was already dark outside, the lamps of the park throwing their yellow glow across the trees and bushes, illuminating the few people still strolling around. If she tried really hard, she could imagine that she was back at Pengarroth Hall, back amongst the scenery, the greenery, might even be able to smell the damp earth, the leaves, the freedom.

Then she turned away decisively. She must stop this daydreaming, she told herself. And she must never go back to Pengarroth Hall. It was safer to stay here, for this was where she belonged, not there. And if Sebastian did get in touch with her again—before the dinner date she'd agreed to—she'd make an excuse, any excuse, not to meet up until then. Distance was the safest thing.

She smiled faintly as she took off her coat. You'd be proud of me, Dad, she thought. Resist all interruptions to worthwhile plans—wasn't that what he always said? It wasn't her fault that Sebastian had turned up last night, or that Mia had invited them to lunch, or that she had been more or less forced to accept the law date with him. None of that was her fault. But not to worry. She'd be careful not to step too far out of line.

CHAPTER ELEVEN

SITTING pensively in front of the mirror in her bedroom as she smoothed body lotion along her neck and shoulders, Fleur anticipated the evening ahead with some misgivings. The night of the law dinner had come all too quickly. She'd tried to put it from her mind.

Two weeks had passed since she and Sebastian had had Sunday lunch with Mia, and during that time Fleur had done her best not to think of him. This had been helped considerably by the fact that there'd been a particularly absorbing project at work, no one leaving the laboratory until eight o'clock for several days running, so that by the time she eventually got home and prepared herself a meal, bed and sleep were all that mattered.

She frowned slightly as her thoughts ran on. Sebastian, too, must have obviously been very occupied, because the only contact he'd made had been one message left on her answering machine, hoping that she was OK, and also that the rest of the painting in her kitchen had gone well. She made a face to herself as she remembered that bit—she'd not had the chance, nor the inclination, to complete the job. It would have to wait until things quietened down at the lab.

Anyway, as far as this evening was concerned, she knew

that the only reason she'd been invited to the event was to act as a decoy for Sebastian. To protect him—how had Mia put it?—from predatory females. Well, that was fine by her. She'd play the part, no problem. And knowing that that was the sole point of her being there would help her to enjoy herself, with no underlying emotional pressures. Her expression cleared. It could prove to be a rather special game of make-believe, she thought, with her and Sebastian the only ones in on the plot. And, afterwards, he could go on his merry way and leave her to go on hers.

His secretary had phoned the night before to explain that he had arranged to send a cab for her at seven o'clock, and exactly on time her doorbell sounded. Picking up her pearl coloured faux fur wrap and a clutch bag, she left the flat and went downstairs. A uniformed chauffeur stood there with the car door already open and, feeling as if she were about to go to a command performance, Fleur picked up the hem of her skirt and got in. Well, that was what this was, she thought—a command performance—though she doubted whether there'd be any red carpet waiting for her.

It took less than half an hour to reach the grand London hotel and, as they pulled up, an official doorman came forward to hand her out of the car. Inside, the brightly-lit and luxurious entrance was thronging with people in full evening dress, and for a second Fleur felt like turning around and running away. She wasn't used to this kind of thing, she thought, and although there had obviously been a few special occasions in her life where everyone had dressed up, they had been few and far between. And they were certainly not her preferred way of spending an evening. But…she'd agreed to come so she'd better make the best of it.

Almost immediately, Sebastian was at her side and as Fleur looked up at him she felt a tremor run right through her. He looked suave, immaculate—and painfully desirable—in a beautifully-cut dinner suit, his hair dark and glossy—and slightly in need of a cut, she thought instinctively, but it suited him like that—and, as usual, with the advantage of his height, he stood head and shoulders above everyone else around. She was aware again of the cut of his jaw, the strength of his shoulders, and as he stood there now, totally relaxed among people he knew and who knew him, she could almost feel the powerful awesomeness which seemed to radiate from him. He smiled down at her, taking her arm and leading her towards the cloakroom.

'Do you want to leave your wrap?' he asked. 'I can assure you that you'll be warm enough in the function room, but perhaps you'd rather hang on to it?'

'No, I'll leave it,' Fleur said.

'Then I'll wait here for you.'

After leaving her wrap with the attendant, Fleur went into the adjoining powder room to take a last look at herself in the mirror. There were several other women there, touching up their make-up, and she could hear the conversation of a few of them who were standing around by the door.

'Well, no one's seen him with anyone,' someone said, 'not for a long time.'

'Doesn't he usually bring his sister?' someone else enquired. 'I liked her—she's a really friendly, bubbly girl.'

'Not like him, then,' was the next remark, and everyone laughed.

'Oh, he's all right,' another one said, 'when you get to know him. Personally, I *like* the strong, silent type. I wouldn't throw him out of bed, that's for sure.'

'Dream on,' said the first girl. 'Anyway, he'll be out of our lives soon, and the place won't seem the same without him. He's going down to the family pile in Cornwall, apparently, to run their estate.' She sighed heavily. 'What a waste of a man—to bury him down there amongst all those pixies and pasties!'

Everyone laughed again as they opened the door to leave, and the parting remark which Fleur heard was, 'Anyway, he's definitely not the marrying kind—not any more.'

'Shh,' someone warned quietly, 'he's standing there outside.'

Fleur stood rooted to the spot. It had been clear to her from the outset that the women had been discussing Sebastian and, although nothing really derogatory had been said, it had made her feel uncomfortable—and defensive—to hear him talked about. And it was also completely understandable why he should not want to come to this function alone, she thought—not if he wanted to avoid unwanted attention.

She left the room and went across to join him. She was going to enjoy carrying out her mission tonight, she thought, and she'd make a good job of it. She'd give those women something to talk about!

Now that he could see her properly, Sebastian made no secret of the fact that he was almost bowled over by her appearance.

'I've never seen you in that colour before,' he murmured slowly, staring down at her. 'It…it really suits you, Fleur.'

'I've only got three good occasion dresses,' she admitted, 'and at first I'd decided to wear my black one, but then I thought everyone would be wearing black. So…' she smiled up at him '…I thought I'd be different.'

The dress was a flame-red, slinky, full-length number, scoop-necked to reveal the slenderness of her neck and shoulders, and the skirt was slit up one side to reveal just enough thigh to be teasingly-seductive as she moved. He noticed that she was wearing slightly more make-up than usual, with the addition of a slick of eye liner and some smoky shadow, and her hair was centre-parted with a lustrous chignon coiled expertly at the back. Her only jewellery seemed to be the same white gold hoop earrings he'd seen on her before, but the whole package was breathtaking—and he knew there'd be plenty of eyes on both of them during the evening. Could this be the next Mrs Sebastian Conway, they'd all be asking themselves, against all the odds? Well, he'd answer that—not a chance. Not because he wasn't interested in her—but because he knew that she wasn't interested in *him*. Charming she certainly was—especially at this moment because he was aware that she'd tucked her small hand into his arm, an unusual act of familiarity on her part. But charm by itself did not equate to feeling anything about someone, he knew that. It was merely a superficial pleasantry. He sighed briefly to himself. He'd better concentrate on this evening—an occasion he usually dreaded rather than looked forward to—and on making sure that Fleur enjoyed herself. He glanced down at her, at the top of her head, at her shining golden hair as they made their way through the crowd… He somehow didn't think it was the sort of event which would appeal to her much, either. In fact, he knew very well where she'd rather be at this moment—tramping through all that wet undergrowth at Pengarroth Hall!

In the crowded reception area, wine was handed around freely and dozens of different conversations soon filled the huge room, everyone talking loudly in order to be heard.

Sebastian introduced Fleur to several people—whose names she knew she'd forget almost immediately. But everyone was chatty and friendly and she smiled happily, thinking what a good thing it was that she was not here as a romantic partner of the man standing so possessively beside her. Because it meant that she could relax totally, without worrying about emotions and feelings. She was here for a practical reason—to ward off unwanted admirers—and just as well, she thought, because she couldn't help noticing the covetous glances directed at Sebastian from time to time. He certainly did need protecting, and there were many attractive, beautifully dressed women he could choose from. But, for a change, she was to be *his* 'minder'—and she was going to make the most of it.

At the signal, they all went into the massive dining room and took their places at one of the round tables, each set for ten people. There were four men and six women on theirs and as they sat down Fleur looked up at Sebastian and smiled provocatively. Let those females without escorts be in no doubt that he was spoken for! And he smiled back, taking her hand and squeezing it gently. He obviously intended to play his part, too!

'Are you OK?' he asked out of the corner of his mouth. 'It's not so good being somewhere among complete strangers, is it…not knowing anyone.'

'But I know you—and that's all that matters,' she replied softly, holding him captive once more with that hesitant, lazy lowering of her eyelids.

Almost at once the small band on the stage began to play in the background, and Fleur automatically tapped her feet in time to the rhythm. She was *glad* she was here—with Sebastian.

It was obviously a very rich gathering, with a mixed age group, she thought, looking around her as the meal was being served. Fleur could only imagine what the tickets for the event must have cost, because success, and the affluence that went with it, was tangible.

'This is one of our main fund-raising events, and I'm glad so many have supported it this evening,' Sebastian told her, as if reading her thoughts. He stopped speaking for a moment while a waiter filled their glasses with sparkling wine. 'We engage an appropriate firm to arrange everything, and they always seem to come up with something special to swell the funds. Last year we did fantastically well—after dinner they set up a mock horse-racing game and everyone gambled.' He drank from his glass. 'We never know what they've planned until the night, but it's usually great fun.'

The man sitting next to Fleur turned towards her for a moment. 'And what do you do in your working life, Fleur?' he enquired politely. 'No, let me guess. You're a famous model…'

Fleur smiled quickly, giving the man brief details in answer to his question, and he was clearly impressed. 'Makes a change from what many of us in this room do all day,' he said. He paused, glancing surreptitiously across at Sebastian, who was talking to the woman on his other side. 'Have you…have you known Sebastian long?' he asked curiously.

'Long enough,' she replied obliquely. Let the man make what he liked of that remark! Poor Sebastian, she thought. His personal life was obviously a matter of great interest to his colleagues. And she could guess how much he must hate it.

The food was good and well-served and after dinner the grand auction began—this year's special event. It got going quickly and with great enthusiasm, and Fleur was amazed at the value of everything. The list of desirable items went on and on, and bidding was fast and furious. Fleur's breath was almost taken away by the speed of everything in the hands of the professional auctioneer, and also by the totals being achieved. She looked up at Sebastian.

'I've never seen anything like this,' she said over the noise in the room, and he smiled at her, obviously pleased at how much money was being raised.

'At this rate, we're going to beat last year's total,' he said, and she realized how genuine his concern was for the charity they were supporting.

The atmosphere in the room had become more and more hectic and excitable, and Fleur's head had begun to spin slightly as her wineglass was regularly refilled. But the expensive alcohol and the food had the effect of totally relaxing her, making her feel almost on another planet as she took in everything that was going on around her. She was overwhelmingly conscious of Sebastian's closeness to her, of how he occasionally leaned forward towards her, putting his arm around her shoulders and drawing her in to him in almost a bear hug as he bid for something enthusiastically.

Finally, everything had been spoken for, with cheques and bank notes being hurriedly counted, and the MC took the microphone.

'Now then, ladies and gents,' he said. 'Tonight, as a somewhat novel slant to the proceedings, I'm going to ask for a volunteer from each table to come up and sing for us. Sing along with the band, I mean—anything you like—and I shall ask the rest of you to bid the money you think each singer is worth.'

A gale of whooping and laughter greeted his words,

followed by shrieks, protests and arguments as people tried to cajole others to volunteer.

Fleur sat back languidly and looked around her at the rest of the table. One of the women would be only too happy to do it, she thought. They'd certainly all been very noisy so far during the evening, if that was anything to go by. But, surprisingly, there was a flat refusal from each one.

'You can count me out,' the tall brunette opposite said. 'Not my scene, thanks.' She looked across at the man sitting next to Fleur. 'How about you, Tom? Music's your thing, isn't it?'

'It is,' he agreed, 'but I only sing in the bath these days.'

Sebastian decided to take charge of proceedings. 'Look, it's only a laugh,' he said reasonably. 'You're not auditioning for the West End. Come on—one of you has to do it.'

'How about you having a go?' someone said. 'I propose Sebastian!'

'Not a chance,' he replied. 'But one of you simply *must*—we can't be the only table not to take part. Come *on*…'

'Oh, dear, Sebastian has spoken,' one of the women said, her words slurring slightly, 'and we all know what *that* can mean…'

Suddenly, as if someone else was speaking for her, Fleur said calmly, 'I'll do it, if you want me to, Sebastian.'

Afterwards, she would never know what had made her volunteer, but the look of relief on Sebastian's face was reward enough.

As the organizers had known, hearing unwilling victims make themselves conspicuous in this way was an inspired idea, and soon there was huge applause and ribald encouragement from the room as each singer took part, all of them crooning lustily to the latest pop number, and with hearty support from the band.

Sebastian's table was the last one to take part, and slowly Fleur got up from her chair, watched with mixed feelings by the other women. Sebastian stood as well and, with his arm held protectively around her waist, he led her up to the stage.

Going across to the keyboard player, Fleur said, almost apologetically, 'I don't really sing pop...but...do you know Mancini's *Moon River*?'

The man smiled up at her. 'Course I do,' he said. 'Lovely number.' And at once he played the introduction to the well-known song.

Feeling again as if she wasn't here at all, but drifting along several feet in the air, Fleur began the first notes of the sad, nostalgic tune, with its evocative lyrics. Almost at once the room fell silent as she sang, with no one calling out or shifting in their seats.... *'Moon River, wider than a mile, I'm crossing you in style, some day...'* her voice, pure and note perfect, echoed wistfully around the room *'...we're after the same rainbow's end, waiting round the bend, my huckleberry friend, moon river...and me.'*

As the last notes died away, there was a complete hush, apart from someone blowing their nose quietly as the wistfulness of the number touched a nerve. This was unexpected, unlike anything else that had been sung, and it had the effect of stunning everyone into momentary silence. But not for long. The reception Fleur got was huge, with some people getting to their feet and shouting for an encore, but at once Sebastian held out his hand to help her off the stage before leading her back to the table.

The money raised exceeded every expectation. Each singer had to stand up to be recognized again as people shouted their bids from all around the room and when Fleur got to her feet the bidding reached a crescendo.

Sebastian leaned towards her to whisper in her ear. 'I think you can safely say you were the hit of the evening, Fleur. And you certainly earned your dinner. Very many thanks for stepping in.' He paused. 'You were…fantastic.' He paused. 'I was…so proud of you.'

Fleur sipped again at her glass, thinking—did I really do that? What came over me? And she realized that it was the first time she'd sung in public for years. And it had seemed such a natural thing for her to do.

Soon, that part of the evening was over and the dancing began, and immediately Sebastian stood up.

'Come on,' he said, as Fleur stood as well, 'it takes someone to start the ball rolling,' and immediately he took her in his arms and together they went onto the dance floor. And as they swayed there together, with Sebastian's arms supporting her firmly, Fleur felt as if this definitely was all a dream. She looked up at him and he gazed into her eyes and suddenly, remembering that she had a job to do, and that they were being watched by more than one or two, she closed her eyes and raised her lips, inviting him to kiss her. He seized the opportunity at once, closing his mouth over her parted lips and holding her captive for several mind-numbing seconds. Suddenly Fleur wasn't acting a part any longer—she was engaged in something far more realistic, far more subtle, far more true to herself. She was doing— allowing Sebastian to do—something which she'd been subconsciously yearning for, and the enormity of that silent admission was almost too much for her. This wasn't the way things were meant to be! Getting involved, getting cornered, how would it all end?

He seemed to sense her sudden tenseness and looked down at her as she pulled away from him. 'What is it? Are you OK?' he asked, not letting her go, still holding her body against his.

'I'm fine,' she answered shakily. 'Just a bit warm, that's all.'

'Then we'll sit down,' he said, leading her by the hand over to the side of the room, where there were some chairs.

Fleur knew she was trembling and, to cover her confusion, she said, 'Well, how am I doing? Am I succeeding in my task for tonight?'

He stared down at her for a second, not understanding what she meant. 'Your task?'

'Am I providing sufficient armour for you against all the women lusting for you, Sebastian? Am I heading them off? Have they got the message?'

Now he did understand her and his expression darkened, his eyes glittering and thoughtful. 'I think I can say that you are fulfilling all the criteria in every particular,' he said slowly. 'And I'm sure I'm the object of much envy amongst my colleagues.' He paused, turning to face her and taking her hand in his. 'But, despite what you may think, you are not here because Mia left you no option, Fleur, but because I wanted you to be here. I wanted your company. I…I wanted *you*…I hope you'll believe that.'

And, looking at him longingly, Fleur did believe that. Because she wanted to believe it. And because she knew that Sebastian Conway did not make such statements lightly. But it did nothing to solve her long-standing problem—that she intended never to tread the same path as her mother had done all her life. Yet where did love, and passion, and physical need come in that plan? Those finer feelings were beginning to become vital components in an existence which had seemed so straightforward and clear-cut before she'd set foot in Pengarroth Hall. Where was she to go from here? she asked herself desperately.

CHAPTER TWELVE

'FLEUR? Hi! Hope I haven't got you out of bed...I just had to ring and find out how you enjoyed last night. Was it fantastic?'

Fleur, still mooning around in her dressing gown sipping a cup of coffee, smiled briefly. She might have known that Mia would want all the details—because she couldn't rid herself of the suspicion that her friend was trying her hand at matchmaking.

'Hi, Mia—yes, it was a very grand affair, and I think a lot of money was raised.'

Mia sighed impatiently. 'Never mind about all that—what did you wear? I bet you looked stunning—and how about my brother? Was he in a "Seb" mood or a "Sebastian Conway" mood?'

'I wore my red dress,' Fleur replied, 'which I don't think you can have seen because I've only worn it once before...' She paused. 'And Sebastian was...' How was she going to put this? Was she going to say that he was the most drop-dead gorgeous man in the room and that he'd been utterly attentive towards her—attentive and charming and so desirable that she'd wanted him to kiss her. Had *invited* him to kiss her right there in the middle of the dance floor with everyone watching! She couldn't possibly say all that—especially as this morning she felt somehow dejected and confused.

'Sebastian was exemplary in every way,' she said neatly.

'What time did it finish?' Mia wanted to know.

'Oh, about one o'clock,' Fleur replied 'Sebastian came home with me in the cab, and then dropped me off.'

There was a pause. 'He didn't spend the night on the sofa bed, then?' Mia asked mischievously.

'He certainly did not,' Fleur replied. 'What made you think that?'

'Oh, just a feeling I had...' Mia said obliquely, then decided not to pursue that train of thought. She knew very well that Fleur was sensitive on the matter of relationships, but she also knew her brother well enough to realize that he liked Fleur—liked her a lot. In fact, she could have put it more strongly than that but thought she wouldn't tempt fate by assuming anything. 'Anyway, I *knew* you'd enjoy yourself—Seb knows how to give a woman a good time,' she said lightly.

They chatted casually for a while, making plans to meet later in the week before hanging up. It was only a few minutes later when the phone rang again. Fleur paused before picking it up... She knew who it would be this time.

'Morning, Fleur. I hope you slept better than I did.'

Sebastian certainly did sound gruff-voiced today, she thought. But that would be the effect of rather too much alcohol. 'I slept well, thanks,' she said. 'In fact, I'm not even up and dressed yet and I feel very lazy.'

There was a pause for a moment, then Sebastian said, 'I just wanted to thank you for...accompanying...me last night, Fleur. I hope you enjoyed yourself.' Well, he knew very well that she'd enjoyed herself—and *he'd* loved every minute of being by her side. And when, unbelievably, she'd stood up on the stage and sung that beautiful song, she had captivated many other hearts beside his own. It had seemed to put the crowning glory on his thoughts about her, demonstrating her gentleness and inherent goodness. She was the sort of woman whom any man would feel happy to trust with his future—qualities which he'd been quick to recognize almost from the moment he'd met her. He knew without a shadow of a doubt that, somehow, he had to convince her that she might be able to commit herself to him without all the nagging doubts and anxieties she clearly had about the opposite sex—her fear of being controlled and manipulated. But he knew he had to be careful. One wrong move too soon, and he'd lose her—it would be like trying to catch a dainty butterfly without crushing a wing, he thought. But he was determined to do it. Determined to succeed.

'I did enjoy myself—very much, thank you, Sebastian,' she replied. 'I…I only hope that making something of an exhibition of myself on stage didn't embarrass you,' she added.

'Not a chance, and I was very impressed. You…you've got a lovely voice, Fleur.'

'Well, anyway, I didn't notice any unwelcome females throwing themselves at you, so at least I must have been of some practical value,' she said.

'I wish you wouldn't think of it like that,' Sebastian said, his voice harsh for a second. 'I told you—I *wanted* you there. And I'm quite able to look out for myself, in any case. I don't need that kind of protection from another human being.'

Fleur was quick to notice the change in his tone. How could anyone think that he wasn't master of the situation—whatever it might happen to be?

'Actually,' he went on, changing the subject, 'I know you said you haven't finished painting your kitchen yet.' He paused. 'How about this afternoon...or maybe one evening in the week? I'm not too busy for a few days, as it happens.'

Fleur sighed inwardly. She knew she could not put him off with any old excuse, and it *was* good of him to offer. She'd better agree, and get it over with. Even if she *had* made up her mind that she wasn't going to see him again.

'I don't think I could face it today, Sebastian,' she said, 'but...next Saturday seems a better option...if you're sure you don't mind.'

'If I minded, I wouldn't be offering,' he said flatly, 'and next Saturday's fine by me too.'

After she'd put the phone down, Fleur stood for a moment, looking out of her bedroom window. She knew it was not going to be easy to keep him at arm's length, even though she told herself that that was the best thing to do. It was hard to be negative and choosy where Sebastian Conway was concerned, especially as she was honest enough to admit that for the first time in several years she felt a growing excitement inside, a feeling of anticipation— a feeling that life had a lot more to offer.

She went into the bathroom and switched on the shower. It was only six days before next Saturday...

'Something smells good,' Sebastian said appreciatively as he followed Fleur into the sitting room. 'See—I've come well prepared this time, brought my own brushes in case yours aren't suitable.'

It was the following Saturday afternoon, and Fleur had already prepared and cooked a curry for them to eat later.

She felt that the least she could do was to offer him supper, and it would be easy to heat the curry up and boil some rice later. She smiled at him.

'I hope you like curry,' she said. 'The one I make is a special recipe given to me by an Indian lady I work with.'

'I like anything—and I certainly like curry.' He went into the kitchen to look around and assess everything. 'I approve of the colour you've chosen,' he said as he examined the pots of paint, 'and the white gloss will look good against it.' He shrugged off his jacket, taking the grimy apron from Fleur, and set to work at once.

'I think decorating is quite a therapeutic occupation,' he said, glancing down at her from the ladder. 'I don't do much of it at Pengarroth Hall, because we usually employ people, and Pat's jolly good at it and often insists on doing the honours.' He stretched upwards, drawing the brush firmly along the expanse of the wall. 'But when I'm living there permanently, I'll have more time. There'll be all sorts of things I'll be able to help out with.'

Fleur went out, leaving him to it—well, he'd get on quicker if she wasn't there, she thought, when suddenly she heard his mobile ring.

'Answer that, Fleur,' Sebastian called. 'The phone's in my coat pocket.'

'Hello, this is Sebastian Conway's number...' Fleur said obediently.

The female voice which answered was quiet and well-modulated, and its owner was obviously surprised not to hear Sebastian. 'Oh...is...is Sebastian there?' There was a moment's hesitation. 'This is his grandmother speaking.'

Sebastian had come into the sitting room, wiping his hands, and he took the phone from Fleur. 'Rose...how lovely to hear from you! How are you…?' There was a pause, then, 'As a matter of fact, I'm doing some decorating for someone at the moment. I was up a ladder when you rang.' He smiled briefly as he listened, then, 'Oh…it's someone called Fleur…Fleur Richardson…she's been staying at Pengarroth Hall recently…yes…no… She's actually a friend of Mia's. Yes…another friend of Mia's. I don't think you've ever met.' He raised his eyes at Fleur apologetically, but didn't interrupt his grandmother again as she continued speaking. Then, 'Oh…yes, I see. Well…' he glanced at his watch '…I could come over later—maybe about six… What? I don't know…I'll ask her but…just a minute…' He put his hand over the mouthpiece. 'My grandmother is begging me to go over to her flat later on because she's got someone staying with her who needs some advice about something.' He frowned briefly. 'I don't like to refuse because the man has been a good friend to our family, and his time's limited because apparently he's flying back to Australia tomorrow.'

'Then you must go,' Fleur said at once. 'The painting can wait, Sebastian. There are more important things in life.'

'Yes, but I've been instructed to bring you as well,' Sebastian said and, as she went to decline, added, 'Please say you'll come, Fleur…'

Fleur hesitated, but only for a moment. 'Oh, go on, then,' she said. 'If you really want me to.' Well, how could she have refused? Sebastian already knew that she was not going anywhere that night.

He raised his thumb at her briefly, telling his grandmother that they'd be there later on, then switched off the phone.

'Really, there's no need for me to be involved,' Fleur said. 'It's you they want to see, Sebastian…'

'On the contrary. As soon as my grandmother knew I was with a young woman, that was it. She insisted that you come too, says she needs livening up. And when Rose has spoken, everyone obeys!' He smiled across at her. 'Actually, you'd like her, Fleur. She's a real character…and…she meant a great deal to me at a certain point in my life.'

'Mia has often spoken to me about her,' Fleur said. 'I always felt quite envious because I never knew my grandparents.'

'Well, I'll be delighted to introduce you to mine. Well, to one of them,' Sebastian said, going back into the kitchen and taking up the paintbrush again. 'Rose is in a class all of her own.'

Fleur watched as the elderly lady leaned forward to pour some sherry into two glasses, before handing one to her and sitting down opposite.

'Now, my dear,' Rose said without preamble. 'With the two men out of the way in the other room talking business, you must tell me all about yourself. You're a friend of Mia's, I understand, rather than a friend of Sebastian's, I mean?'

Fleur smiled inwardly. The significance of the remark was not lost on her. It was obvious that Rose thought there might be more to this than met the eye. But it was impossible not to warm to the old lady. She was a handsome, tall and elegant woman, her abundant silver-grey hair swept on top in a knot, and with her slender figure, immaculate make-up and pearl nail polish she reminded Fleur of one of the veteran actresses regularly seen in television dramas. She was wearing a cashmere dress in the softest lavender, and on her feet were smart high-heeled black patent leather shoes. The complete picture of a well-to-do lady, Fleur thought.

'I suppose I'm a friend of them both,' she replied in answer to Rose's question, 'though of course I've known Mia a lot longer because we were at school together.' She sipped from her glass. 'I was very kindly invited to stay at Pengarroth Hall for Christmas, and for a while after that…and Sebastian was there as well, so we do know each other a little better now…'

Rose nodded, her clear blue eyes fixed thoughtfully on Fleur, and although this might normally have made the girl feel uncomfortable, somehow it didn't. She couldn't help feeling perfectly at ease.

'Tell me what you do…where you live, Fleur. And you must forgive me for my questioning…but other people's lives are so much more interesting than one's own, don't you think? Especially when one is older.'

Fleur found herself explaining everything about herself, surprised at how uninhibited she was feeling. She wasn't usually this relaxed with strangers.

'So you see,' she concluded at last, 'Mia and I go back a long way, and she is the best friend anyone could have. I value her friendship so much.'

'And how did you get on with my grandson? I know he can be…difficult…sometimes.' Rose's question demanded an answer! 'I worry about him a little.'

'Sebastian has been very kind to me,' Fleur said at once. 'I was made extremely welcome in Cornwall, and I think they've got the most beautiful estate. And Pat, too, was lovely to me. I had a great time.'

Rose sighed briefly and leaned back in her chair for a moment. 'It's just that Sebastian is sometimes misjudged by people who don't know him, and I want him to be happy. To be understood. I want people to like him— because he deserves to be liked.'

'I don't think that *I* find him difficult to understand,' Fleur began.

Rose went on, 'He was always a complete mystery to his parents, you know, because he *was* a bit wild in his younger days.' She paused. 'But he was—and I'm sure still is—very idealistic, and could never see why some people appear to have so much of this world's goods, and others not. He disliked the idea of inherited wealth, you see. Then, just when he left university, he disappeared—for two whole months! Can you believe it? Nearly drove his mother potty! He left a note saying that they weren't to worry, that he was perfectly all right, but that he needed to be by himself to think things over.' Rose took another sip from her glass, while Fleur listened with growing interest. Yes, Sebastian *was* a complex character, she thought.

'Where…where did he go…where had he been?' she asked tentatively.

'No one ever knew exactly,' Rose said, 'but he told us afterwards that he'd been sleeping rough. Here, there and everywhere. Wanted to see for himself what it really meant to have nothing. To have to live by your wits. And that's apparently what happened, and I don't suppose it did him any harm because when he came back he finished his law education and settled down. Mind you, my dear—' Rose leaned forward conspiratorially '—I don't think he imagined he'd have the running of Pengarroth Hall quite so soon…terrible shock that his parents—my son and his wife—died so unexpectedly.' She sighed, looking pensive for a moment, and Fleur admitted to suddenly feeling sad for Sebastian. To have so much, yet not to be free.

'Sebastian and I have always been close,' Rose went on, 'because we seem to tick in much the same way.' She paused. 'When my husband and I got married and he first took me to live at Pengarroth Hall I thought I'd die at the very thought of it! The idea of being lady of the manor didn't appeal at all!' She looked rueful for a moment. 'I'm a city girl at heart and, although I did learn to appreciate all the beauty of the place, London was where I yearned to be for much of the time. Isn't that a dreadful thing to say? Most people would much prefer the country life. And I know Sebastian feels resentful sometimes, at the lot which has fallen on him.'

Just then, Sebastian and the visitor emerged from the other room and, presently after a few more minutes' chatting, Sebastian took Fleur by the arm, looking at his grandmother fondly.

'I'm sorry we can't join you for supper, Rose,' he said, 'because someone has already prepared a meal for us, and we can't disappoint them. But—' he paused, looking down at Fleur for a second '—I promise to bring Fleur back to see you soon.'

'Please do, Sebastian,' Rose said. 'We've had a lovely chat, Fleur and I, and you know how much I need you young things to keep *me* feeling young. And I want to hear all about the Christmas festivities at Pengarroth Hall. Mia told me some of it on the phone, but I'm sure there's lots I haven't heard!'

Driving back to her flat, Sebastian glanced across at Fleur. 'You're subdued,' he said and, when she didn't answer, added, 'What did you think of Rose?'

'I think she is absolutely lovely,' Fleur replied. 'Why don't you call her Grandmother, by the way?'

He waited a second before answering. 'Because I don't often think of her as that,' he said slowly. 'She's always been someone I could talk to—as a friend rather than a relation—and, anyway, I think Rose suits her perfectly. I think she has to be the most glamorous granny in the world.' He drummed his fingers on the steering wheel as they waited for the traffic lights to turn green. 'I hope my little fib about going on somewhere for supper was OK with you.' He turned to glance across at her. 'But I couldn't bear the thought of that curry going to waste.' He didn't add that he couldn't bear the thought of sharing her with others for a moment longer.

Fleur smiled without looking back at him. 'Of course it was OK with me,' she said. 'Anyway, there's the painting to finish.'

It was much too late to do any more painting that night and presently when they'd eaten their supper and shared half a bottle of wine, Sebastian stood up. He was not going to put Fleur in the position of inviting him to stay the night on the sofa bed again, because he had the distinct feeling that the cards were beginning to fall in his favour. It was just a feeling, he told himself, but it would do for now. And caution was advisable!

He held out his hands, taking both of hers and pulling her up towards him. 'I must go, Fleur,' he said softly. 'But I'll be back tomorrow and finish that kitchen if it kills me.'

'I don't want you to do anything that might kill you,' she replied, 'because…' She didn't go on, she couldn't go on, because now his lips were fusing with hers, the warmth of their bodies melding until it felt as if they were one person sharing an exhilarating thrill of passionate longing. Her lips were parted, her white teeth gleaming in the subdued light, and Fleur suddenly felt a terrifying thrill that her principles, her determination, were at risk of being blown away. She let him hold her there like that, not wanting to pull away, not wanting this to stop.

But it did. And it was Sebastian who stopped it.

'I must go, Fleur,' he repeated softly. 'But I'll be back tomorrow. Early.'

She closed the door behind him, waiting until she heard his car pull away from the street before going back inside and throwing herself down on the sofa. She was trembling all over with suppressed desire, and this self-knowledge both delighted and shocked her. After a few moments, her heart-rate lessened and she began to calm down. She knew very well that if Sebastian had asked to share her bed that night, she would have agreed with not a moment's hesitation. And she didn't know whether to laugh or cry!

CHAPTER THIRTEEN

THE next day—without any further interruptions—Sebastian made short work of what remained to be done in Fleur's kitchen. Finally, at about four o'clock, he stood back and viewed his handiwork complacently.

'Well, although I say it myself, that looks pretty good to me,' he said.

'And I second that,' Fleur said as, with her arms folded, she stood in the doorway admiring his efforts. 'See what happens when you turn up unexpectedly? You didn't know what you would be letting yourself in for, did you?'

He glanced across at her as he began putting everything away. 'As I said, I rather enjoy decorating—in small doses.' He replaced the lid firmly on one of the paint tins. 'But I think I'm going to be ready for some supper later.'

Fleur had prepared some filled rolls for their lunch and she had to admit that she, too, would enjoy something a bit more exciting. 'We'll walk to the little Italian place around the corner—I think you'll like it,' she said.

After Sebastian had showered and put on the fresh shirt he'd brought with him, they sat together with a drink in their hands. Fleur looked across at him apologetically.

'Before we eat, Sebastian, I feel the desperate need for

a walk amongst some trees—but you needn't come,' she said. 'There aren't many evenings when I don't have a stroll in the park—whatever the weather. And there wasn't a chance yesterday, was there?'

'Of course I'll come,' Sebastian said at once, his eyes narrowing briefly. Perhaps out there amongst the natural surroundings which she so obviously loved, he would find the opportunity to ask her a rather important question—something which had been on his mind for some time.

They made their way to the entrance of the park and Sebastian pushed open the big iron gate. A light rain had begun to fall and it was almost dark, the overhead lights already throwing their guiding beams along the winding paths as they strolled along. Fleur looked up at him.

'I must have walked the length and breadth of this place hundreds of times,' she said. 'It's my bolt-hole in times of stress and strain!'

He gazed back down at her. The hood of her jacket had slipped from her head and now there were dozens of tiny rain droplets glistening amongst the waves of her hair. At that moment he could easily have said, *Well, if you would agree to come and live with me in Cornwall, you could have as many walks as you like, each and every day*. But he was still unsure of Fleur, unsure of what her reaction would be, and he knew he must tread carefully. In spite of their passionate embrace last night, in spite of the delectable sensation of her moist lips on his, almost inviting him to seduce her, he felt undeniably wary. It was a new experience for him—because she was unlike any other woman he had ever met, and he would have to use a little cunning if he was to get his own way. Which he knew he was going to, in the end. He cleared his throat.

'I've been meaning to…to ask you something, Fleur,' he began hesitantly, and she looked up at him again quickly, sensing that this was something important! But how important?

'Oh…what's that?' she asked lightly, looking away.

'Of course…I don't expect an answer straight away,' he said quickly, 'because you'll naturally need time to think it over…but it's something I've had on my mind ever since I met you.' He paused, and Fleur's heart jumped in her chest like a nervous kitten. He was going to ask her to marry him! Heaven help her—what was she going to say? Wasn't he just the sort of man—insanely desirable though he was— that she'd promised herself to avoid at all costs? His whole personality shouted importance, determination, authority! Yet, above all that, she knew that she was helplessly in love with him—in love with him so much that her need, her longing for him was becoming a physical pain. She tried to breathe steadily, to calm herself so that when she was forced to respond to his proposal her voice would be steady.

'I don't think you can guess what I'm going to say,' he went on, 'but it would mean a great deal to me if you would agree.'

'Well,' Fleur replied carefully, 'until I know what it is, I can't promise anything, can I…?'

Would he go down on one knee on the wet grass? Somehow she didn't think so!

'I've had a brilliant idea for an event at Pengarroth Hall, which I think would go down well with everyone in the area,' he said, 'and which would be very profitable. But I need someone like you to help me make it work.'

Fleur stared at him uncomprehendingly. What was this all about? He wasn't asking her to marry him, after all!

How could she have *thought* such a thing? He wasn't the marrying kind and never would be! She swallowed hard and kept walking—just a small step in front of him. To say that she felt as if she were standing on the edge of a big hole, about to fall right down to the bottom, would be putting it mildly! Serve her right—her stupid imagination had led her horribly astray! She tried to suppress a painful lump in her throat. 'Go on,' she said quietly, feeling almost limp with disappointment.

'I want to stage a summer musical extravaganza in the grounds. There's a perfect spot for it beyond the kitchen garden at the back of the house. It's a kind of natural auditorium, with a raised area perfect for a stage. These summer spectaculars are being done all over the country at the moment, and the money raised for charity can be fantastic! I'd want a full orchestra, singers, a real production with lighting and amplification—and of course I've got a huge advantage in knowing Rudy.' He paused, looking down at her, but Fleur had fixed her gaze straight ahead.

'What…what has he to do with it?' she asked. 'And, more importantly, what's it to do with *me*?'

'Because I'd want *you* to be the star attraction, of course,' he said in a way that suggested she should have known that straight away. 'You'd be perfect, Fleur. You look wonderful, you've got natural stage presence…and your voice, well, people couldn't stop talking about you after your performance at the dinner.' He stopped walking now and, taking her arm, turned her towards him, forcing her to look up. 'What do you think of the idea? Will you back me? Because I couldn't do it without you. I don't think I'd want to do it without you.'

Fleur's throat was so dry she couldn't even swallow

and she was feeling so let down, so ridiculous, she could hardly bring herself to answer.

'And…Rudy Malone…?' she asked, the thought of ever having to meet the man again filling her with disgust.

'Rudy will be ecstatic about it,' Sebastian said at once. 'I know he can be a pain in some circumstances, but he's amazing at what he does. His London productions are always brilliant—he frequently gets awards. I'll only have to say the word and then leave the rest to him.'

For a moment, Fleur felt angry—and disillusioned. How could Sebastian ask this of her—especially after the way his friend had behaved at Christmas. It was unthinkable that she was going to go along with it… And it seemed to her that Sebastian was obsessed with raising money for charity. It seemed to be the main thing on his mind. Probably helps his conscience deal with his own wealth, she thought. Well, he could find someone else to sing for him!

They walked on in silence for a few moments, Fleur having difficulty in not bursting into tears. If she'd been given this opportunity by anyone else, at another time, she thought—the chance to do some real singing, to actually perform those famous arias that she knew so well with a proper orchestra—she'd have jumped at it! But this scenario was different—and it was cruel! If she agreed, it would mean being in close proximity with a man she detested—and also with the man whom she'd come to love, but who clearly didn't love her. It was an impossible, hopeless proposition.

'I'm not sure that I could find the time, Sebastian,' she said slowly. 'These things can't be thrown together any old how. There would have to be countless rehearsals, total commitment. I do have my work to think about.' She paused to pick up a small branch that had fallen across the path. 'But it was kind of you to think of me,' she added. 'I'm sure you'll be able to find someone else only too ready to step in.'

Now he stopped her again, and this time his arms were around her waist so that she was forced to look up into his face. 'I'm not being kind,' he said gruffly. 'I'm being practical.' He paused. 'And I think I know the real reason you won't do it… It's Rudy, isn't it, Fleur? You're afraid he'll be a nuisance.'

Fleur had difficulty restraining her impatience. He didn't have a clue! she thought. But he'd given her the perfect excuse. Because she could hardly say, *No, Sebastian, it's you. You're the problem. And I must not be near to you, ever again. Knowing you has put me in a dangerous situation—a situation that I don't really know how to handle. Prolonging our association into the summer will only make things worse—much worse. How could I bear it, knowing that I mean nothing to you? I'm just someone who you enjoy kissing now and again.*

She sighed. 'Yes, it is Rudy Malone,' she lied. 'I would not willingly spend even half an hour in his company— unless I had police protection.' She tried to smile, and suddenly Sebastian could bear it no longer. What had made him use this cheap trick? he asked himself. Even though his ambition to stage a musical event on the estate was genuine enough. Why didn't he ask the woman to marry him, and be done with it? Why did he feel the need to get round her like this?

He was holding her close to him and the warmth of her body mingled with his own, filling him with a surging tide of emotion. 'You wouldn't need police protection,

Fleur,' he said softly. 'My protection is all you'll need. That's a promise.'

She frowned slightly, beginning to regain something of her composure now that her position was clear. He could say what he liked, but this would be the last time that she and Sebastian Conway would hold each other close, she thought. She would not see him again, whatever Mia said or did. This was it. And it was good to have come to that decision. Her other life—the life she'd led before she'd met him—was so simple. So uncomplicated. Just the way she wanted it.

'But you couldn't—wouldn't—be there all the time,' she said slowly. 'How could you be? Your own life is as full as mine.'

Unable to stop himself for another second, he bent his head and claimed her lips—and she made no effort to stop him. Her open eyes were wide and misty, and he pulled away slightly, raising his hand and tracing the tender curve of her cheek with his finger. Then he held her again in a close embrace, resting his chin on the top of her head for a moment. 'If you will agree to another minor proposition of mine,' he murmured, 'I give you my word that you'll have all the protection you'll ever need.'

Mystified, Fleur eased away from him and looked up. And, before she could respond, she heard the words she'd lost all hope of ever hearing.

'Will you marry me, Fleur?' His voice was husky, deep with meaning. 'I'm asking you to be my wife. To come and live with me in Cornwall, for ever…' He trailed off, not wanting to hear her refusal, and for the second time in the last half hour Fleur felt her knees tremble, felt her whole body go limp. Only now it wasn't disillusionment that was the cause, but an overwhelming feeling that her heart was about to take flight and leave her body altogether! He *did* want her… He'd just said so! But…there was something he *hadn't* said, something which she'd never heard her father once say to her mother, in all the years they'd been together. And if Sebastian didn't say it, couldn't say it, then she knew what her answer would be.

'Why do you want me to marry you, Sebastian?' she said coolly. 'Is it because Mia would like it…or because it's obvious that I do love Pengarroth Hall and all the people who work there, and would obviously fit in very well. Or perhaps you think I'd be a suitable person to provide an heir to take your place one day? Which is it, I wonder, Sebastian?'

He'd listened without interrupting her and now his face appeared drawn, almost sculpted in the dim light as he listened to her thoughtfully.

'It's none of those things,' he said. He paused, and Fleur waited breathlessly for what might—or might not—come. 'It's because I love you,' and his tone of voice left her in no doubt that he meant it—really meant it. 'I have loved you for as long as I've known you, Fleur. I can't help it if you don't believe me, but that's the truth.'

Oh but she did believe it! Fleur's arms went around his neck and she pulled him towards her, nestling her face in his neck, loving that same manly fragrance that inflamed her every time he came near her. 'Then…I will marry you,' she whispered. 'I will marry you, Sebastian.'

With a huge shudder he tightened his grasp of her until the breath nearly left her body. 'I can't believe it,' he murmured, burying his face in her hair. 'I didn't dare think you'd agree…especially when I knew how you felt about the male sex.' He lifted her face and kissed her again gently.

'And I don't know what you feel about nuptial agreements, but this is my side of the bargain. I give you my solemn promise that your life will always be under your own control. Anyway, I'm going to have enough to think about without butting in on your hopes and dreams...'

Fleur looked up at him, at the sensuous mouth, the firm chin, the wide forehead with those faint worry lines between his dark, mesmerizing eyes. 'I've got the strangest feeling that my hopes and dreams are going to be exactly the same as yours,' she said.

With their arms around each other's waists like two children, they walked along the deserted paths, not wanting these magical moments to pass. But Fleur knew that she must know something...that, if she didn't, it would be between them for the rest of their lives. But how would he take it? She glanced up at him.

'Sebastian...' She paused. 'Tell me about Davina...'

'Ah, yes, Davina,' he said without hesitation. 'You've obviously been told about her.'

'All I've heard—from Mia, and from Pat—is that you were nearly married to her and then suddenly it was all off. Why, Sebastian? What happened?' If he was offended at her curiosity, then it was too bad. This was something she *had* to know about because it had obviously been an overwhelmingly upsetting occurrence at the time—upsetting for others beside himself.

'When I met Davina,' he said, 'I was impressed with her vitality, her enthusiasm for the business she ran—and, of course, she was also very...attractive.' He paused. 'She had made something of herself despite having had no special advantages—no family background or support. And I admired that.' He waited before going on. 'But she was always very evasive about what she actually did. She told me at first that she ran a dress agency, and I believed her. Supposedly selling second-hand designer clothes. I'm not into ladies' fashions so it was unknown territory to me. Well, we were weeks away from the wedding when one of my colleagues—who I introduced Davina to—informed me that he had…availed…himself of her services a few months earlier. Said he thought I really ought to know about it. It turned out that she was running a very successful escort agency—and her fees for her own personal services were exorbitant.' Sebastian cleared his throat, obviously hating having to recall that time. 'My colleague was able to give me plenty of details…'

Fleur didn't look at him as he spoke. What an unbelievable discovery for him to have made—about a woman whom he had loved.

As if reading her thoughts, he went on, 'But, luckily for me, I was able to recover from the blow almost immediately—which rather suggests that my feelings for Davina must have been somewhat superficial. I admit that I was taken in by her, but her dishonesty about it all was harder to bear than knowing that she was happy to sell herself to any man who was prepared to pay.' He waited before going on, then looked down at Fleur solemnly. 'I want a wife who is prepared to be mine, and mine alone,' he said. 'It's one area where I do not believe in sharing.'

'I've no idea what my parents are going to think,' Fleur said as they drew up outside the family home in Sebastian's car.

'I rather hope they'll be pleased for us,' Sebastian said mildly. 'Surely they didn't expect that their beautiful daughter would stay single for ever?'

Fleur thought—never mind what *they* might have expected—her present situation had come as a surprise—a very happy and exciting surprise—to her! She could still hardly believe that Sebastian had asked her to be his wife—or that she had accepted. But when they'd rung Mia to tell her, the phone had almost exploded with her reaction.

'I knew it, I just *knew* it!' she'd cried. 'We'd all hoped for it—Pat and Beryl and Gran—we've been sending hopeful messages to the stars! When's the wedding—and what am I going to wear?'

In spite of Fleur's misgivings, Philip and Helen received the news with obvious pleasure, although Philip was slightly more guarded in his enthusiasm.

'Well, no doubt you can come to some arrangement with the hospital, to continue your research on a part-time basis,' he said. 'That sort of thing is done a lot nowadays, so as not to waste valuable people and their education. It should be simple enough.'

Fleur and Sebastian exchanged glances, and Sebastian said at once, 'I think Fleur will know exactly what's best, Philip. We can trust her to do the right thing.'

Helen's eyes had not stopped shining since she'd heard the news, and she held her daughter's hands tightly. 'I'm so pleased for you, darling,' she said softly. 'I can only hope that you will be as happy as Daddy and I have been.'

Fleur stared at her mother for a moment and thought that perhaps she'd been wrong all the time. Perhaps her mother had been happy after all. Happy to love and care for the man she'd married, whatever his failings. She shrugged inwardly. It was wrong to judge other people's lives when you didn't really know all the facts, she thought.

It was as they were driving back to her flat that Fleur's

hand suddenly went to her throat anxiously, and she looked across at Sebastian.

'Sebastian—there's just one thing… It's something I really cannot agree to, so we'd better sort it out now, straight away…' she began.

Sebastian nearly swerved off the road at her words, but he recovered quickly. 'What…what the hell is that?' he demanded. 'You…you're not changing your mind…?'

'No, no of course not!' Fleur smiled across at him reassuringly. 'It's about the wedding…'

'What about the wedding?'

'Well, I know that… I know your family expects grand affairs and big celebrations and everything but…but I honestly could not bear it. Can we…can we just have a small ceremony, Sebastian—and maybe a party later? When it's all gone quiet? I don't want a fuss. I really couldn't stand it.'

Sebastian blew through his teeth in relief. 'I was wondering what on earth you were going to say,' he replied. 'And I agree with you entirely, Fleur.' He put his hand on her knee and held it there. 'The only people at our wedding are going to be you and me, of course, your parents, and Mia and Rose. And can Pat and Beryl—and Frank—come too? Would you agree to them all being there? I'd hate to leave any of them out—they'd be so hurt.'

Fleur felt a rush of pleasure at his words. He was such a softie, she thought. 'I'd want them there too,' she said. 'All of them. That would be just perfect.'

Two weeks later they drove back to Cornwall and were met at the door by Pat, who immediately burst into tears and threw her arms around Fleur.

'Since you rang with the news we've hardly slept a

wink!' she exclaimed. 'We're so happy, Fleur.' She looked
up at Sebastian. 'And you're a lucky chap, Sebastian.'

He grinned down at her. 'Don't you think I know that, Pat?'

Later that evening, hand in hand, Fleur and Sebastian
walked slowly along the well-loved wooded paths of
Pengarroth Hall. And it was raining.

'I'm beginning to smell spring in the air,' Fleur said
happily. 'It'll be wonderful to be here when it's warm and
sunny—just as wonderful as it is when it's cold and dismal!'

Sebastian put his arm around her waist. 'There's something I want you to see,' he said quietly, and in a few
moments they came to a spot which Fleur immediately recognized. 'Oh, this is where...' she began, for this was
where Benson had lain down and refused to obey her. The
tree trunk she had sat down on as she'd waited for the dog
to get up was still in the same place...

And there, on a small mound in the turf, stood a neatly
carved wooden cross with one word burned into it. 'Benson'
was all it said, and Fleur stopped in her tracks as if she'd
been struck by lightning, her hand going to her mouth.

'Young Martin—Frank's son—made this for Benson,'
Sebastian said. 'He's going to be a fine carpenter one day.'
He paused. 'And he's made a good job of this, hasn't he?'

Fleur had difficulty in speaking, but after a moment she
said, 'It's beautiful, really beautiful, Sebastian. Just like the
beautiful dog who's resting here.'

The quiet family wedding was held on the first day of
spring, and exactly nine months later Alexander Sebastian
Philip Conway was born at Pengarroth Hall, with Pat
happily assisting the doctor while Sebastian held his wife's
hand tightly. And although Sebastian had been undeniably

proud to hold his baby in his arms for a few moments, his main focus had been on Fleur as she lay on the huge bed, her hair spread out in soft damp waves on the pillows, her eyes moist and glistening.

'I didn't know what real happiness was until I met you,' he whispered in her ear. 'Or what it could mean, until I saw our baby being born.'

Fleur squeezed his hand. 'Do you think he'll like us?' she said.

'I know he'll like *you*,' Sebastian replied. 'How could he help himself?'

A few days later, Philip and Helen came to see their first grandchild and, with Mia there as well, they all sat down-stairs in silent admiration as the baby was passed from one to the other. And the bouquets of flowers kept coming and coming until the house was filled with colour and perfume.

'Who's that one from?' Fleur asked as Sebastian took yet another bouquet from Pat as she brought it into the sitting room. He examined the label and smiled, looking across at his wife.

'It's from Rudy, Fleur. He says, "Many congrats and I've booked the last week of August next year for our first pro-duction."' He passed the flowers back to Pat. 'I told you there'd be no stopping him,' he added.

'This is one of the very best days of my entire life,' Helen said softly. It was her turn to hold the baby. 'An un-forgettable day. All my dreams have come true.'

But it was Philip's reaction which astonished Fleur. He seemed besotted with his first grandchild, couldn't stop gazing down at the sleeping child and saying things like 'What a grand little chap,' and 'Do you think he looks a bit like me, Helen…his nose, I mean?'

At which point Mia had interrupted firmly, 'I think his nose is *exactly* like mine…'

But then Philip said, 'I wonder if Alexander is going to conquer the world some day, to help push scientific knowledge forward a step or two…or maybe he'll become a famous lawyer whose services everyone wants.' He glanced across at Sebastian for a second, before adding, 'I wonder what life has in store for you, Alexander.'

Sebastian went over to sit next to Fleur, slipping his arm around her shoulders for a second. 'Whatever it is, Philip, he'll make the best of it, like we all must do. But it'll be up to him, and it'll be his choice—with, I hope, a little guidance from his parents,' he added.

And Fleur, snuggling into Sebastian and looking around the room at all the people she loved best in the world, thought that wherever paradise eventually turned out to be, at this moment it was very definitely right here, on earth.

2 FREE

BOOKS AND A SURPRISE GIFT!

We would like to take this opportunity to thank you for reading this Mills & Boon® book by offering you the chance to take TWO more specially selected titles from the Modern™ series absolutely FREE! We're also making this offer to introduce you to the benefits of the Mills & Boon® Book Club™—

- ★ **FREE home delivery**
- ★ **FREE gifts and competitions**
- ★ **FREE monthly Newsletter**
- ★ **Exclusive Mills & Boon Book Club offers**
- ★ **Books available before they're in the shops**

Accepting these FREE books and gift places you under no obligation to buy, you may cancel at any time, even after receiving your free shipment. Simply complete your details below and return the entire page to the address below. You don't even need a stamp!

YES! Please send me 2 free Modern books and a surprise gift. I understand that unless you hear from me, I will receive 4 superb new titles every month for just £3.19 each, postage and packing free. I am under no obligation to purchase any books and may cancel my subscription at any time. The free books and gift will be mine to keep in any case.

P9ZED

Ms/Mrs/Miss/Mr .... Initials ....

BLOCK CAPITALS PLEASE

Surname ....

Address ....

....

.... Postcode ....

Send this whole page to:
UK: FREEPOST CN81, Croydon, CR9 3WZ

Offer valid in UK only and is not available to current Mills & Boon Book Club subscribers to this series. Overseas and Eire please write for details and readers in Southern Africa write to Box 3010, Pinegowie, 2123 RSA. We reserve the right to refuse an application and applicants must be aged 18 years or over. Only one application per household. Terms and prices subject to change without notice. Offer expires 30th September 2009. As a result of this application, you may receive offers from Harlequin Mills & Boon and other carefully selected companies. If you would prefer not to share in this opportunity please write to The Data Manager, PO Box 676, Richmond, TW9 1WU.

Mills & Boon® is a registered trademark owned by Harlequin Mills & Boon Limited.
Modern™ is being used as a trademark. The Mills & Boon® Book Club™ is being used as a trademark.